Abducted By
Aliens & Off Planet

(Book 2 of The Abducted Saga)

Please read: Abducted and in an Asylum, Book 1 first.

K.S. Riggin

Table of Contents

Prelude

Conversations with Carthian:

"Abducted? You were never abducted by aliens. You are now among us, your own people." the Dirzaght Carthian tells me.

"No, that's wrong," I explain, shaking my head. *"My whole life, I've been abducted by aliens: the Dirzaght, the Prezvaght, my uncle, and a score of human psychiatrists. Can't you see, they've all held me in a kind of torpor, a stasis of indecision and loss of self."*

"Then you must pull yourself out. It is as simple as that," he says.

Chapter One

"Kaipor? Where are you?" I call out softly, then repeat with the mind link.

My call falls flat in the chill of the morning air. I shiver as I slip my feet into the house slippers and throw the robe around my shoulders.

Kaipor, please answer me. Are you okay?

He cannot answer. He is back on Dirzaght, says a voice from the other side of the room. I turn and gape. It's a stranger, an alien from Dirzaght.

He snorts a chuckle. *How can I be an alien, child, when I am the same species as you?*

I close my mouth, not sure how to answer that. I want to demand the reason this stranger is in my bedroom, but something stops me. I have the feeling that it would be rude to question his presence.

Instead I ask, *Why did Kaipor go back to Dirzaght? Is he hurt?*

Don't be foolish. Of course, he is not hurt. He is Dirzaght. However, he is in trouble. He did things without permission. The Council is very angry.

But he saved me. That man was going to . . .

Yes, I know — shameful lack of common courtesy — an injustice without merit. However, your travmeb exceeded his rights. The Council doesn't appreciate interference, any interference, no matter how warranted, and what Kaipor did was extraordinarily bad. He will be punished severely.

No! That's wrong. What can I do?

The man steps closer. His silver skin shines softly in the stray sunbeams that filter through the blinds. When he blinks, I see the Dirzaght eyes, familiar to me from Kaipor's constant presence.

Do you really want to save him? Are you that content with your travmeb?

Of course. I love him.

I forget there's a stranger in my bedroom and that I'm wearing only a nightgown. I bolt out of bed, somehow feeling that standing upright will aid my case.

Good. Then you will come with me. I will return you to Dirzaght. You must plead your case before the High Ones. It will take that to save Kaipor from the tortures of Estire.

Tortures? I cringe. *They torture people on Dirzaght?* I writhe my hands, not like Pontius Pilate regretting his decision to crucify Christ, but with the twisting hands of worry. What have I done to Kaipor? What are they doing to him?

No, it is not as I see in your thoughts. We have no stretching racks or whips that damage the body. Only punishments of endurance.

I am uncertain what that means. Although it's a relief, he won't be physically tortured . . .

Let me get dressed then, I say, turning to grab some jeans.

No time. Take my hand. We go now.

The High Ones later tell me that I was foolish to place my trust so easily just because the one who'd come for me was Dirzaght. But what do I know? I tell them that, but they find my response hilarious. They laugh and laugh but do not explain.

Still, when I arrive, they do not rebuke me outright for coming to see them. In fact, they welcome me into their embrace, showering me with presents and acknowledgements. First they feed me dainty sweets, fruits so delicious I cannot get enough of them, breads with nuts, and for dessert, something green I *could* live without.

When our meal is finished, they entreat me to bathe in a tub larger than an Olympic swimming pool, without any smell of chlorine! In fact, everywhere, the fragrance in the air is an utter delight: ginger, sugar cookies, lemon, and vanilla. I'm not sure how they complement each other, but they do. I breathe in so deeply that I grow high off the scents.

After soaking in the warm, bubbly waters, I find that the women have replaced my nightgown with a comfortable pastel yellow gown that drapes me modestly and feels like silk against my skin.

One of the High Ones combs my hair, another trims my nails, then a third paints them with shiny apricot polish. I wonder if a fourth will brush my teeth, but although they giggle at the thought, I am handed a soft toothbrush, exactly like the kind we have on Earth, except the toothpaste is already part of the toothbrush. The flavor is delicious.

I ask them about shoes because all I had with me are my bunny slippers. Those don't suit my dress. Lots of head shakes and tsks accompany my request for footwear. Apparently, shoes are not worn by the Dirzaght. My Earth mom would have been appalled.

After the eating, bathing, and primping rituals, I am led into a large hall where cushy chairs are arranged in a circle. Glancing about, I see that all the ladies are wearing gowns like mine. They're all barefoot, too.

I figure the circle is the place I will learn about where Kaipor has been taken, but every time I bring up his name, I am shushed. The conversation weaves all around me, but I learn nothing new. It's as if they've arranged for a discussion of trivia. Of course, I'm not really language proficient in Dirzaght. Sometimes, the conversation just leaves me yawning, and I realize I've lost track of it. But no one seems upset that I don't take an active part. I think they expect it.

After the group discussion ends, two young women lead me to a room with a thick quilt on the floor. Although it has no mattress, the bed feels like how I'd always imagined lying on clouds would feel.

My pillow is shaped like an octopus, except for having only four tentacles instead of eight. It frightens me when its arms surround my neck, but then I realize the tentacles are only puffing outwards, readjusting for maximum comfort. I sleep without dreams that night, or at least any that I can remember, sunk deep in the land of Hypnos.

In the morning, the two women who accompanied me the night before offer me my dress choice of colors. All the dresses are rolled up bundles inside a chest of drawers at the far side of the room. I glance around the room and see no closet, no place to hang anything.

I pick out a light blue gown but wonder if it will be too creased to wear. I slip it over my head, realizing I have no other choice since even my nightgown is gone. As the gown accommodates itself to my body, it falls softly to my ankles, not a wrinkle in sight.

I am comfortable in the dress, and I know it's very pretty, but I'd trade it easily for the security of jeans and a tee shirt. More than once, such tomboy wear, as my mom used to call it, has saved me from the sharp barbs of life's arrows. Yet, I say nothing to the women, for they are generous with me. I do halt them before they can tie a big, blue bow in my hair. *Enough with the primping,* I think at them, and they break into giggles.

I have come to save Kaipor, my *travmeb*, a relationship I think is rather like Earth's husband and wife. Kaipor was taken away to be tortured, according to the Dirzaght male who brought me here. That was because my *travmeb* had defended me against a rapist.

All that morning, I keep explaining to the High Ones that Kaipor's rescue is my sole reason for visiting, but they wave their hands about, and tell me not to worry. That goes on day after day.

Finally, I can't take it anymore. "I will go to the Council, myself, if you won't help me," I threaten, raising my voice louder than is polite in the hope of displaying my urgency.

"How dare you speak so sharply to us," one says, her voice *literally* dropping crystals from the ceiling.

"She is young," says another, whose snow-white skin is like a beautifully carved ice sculpture.

"She is in love," speaks a third — she who has been like a mother since I arrived. She is one of the two women who has helped me dress and has been giving me tips on acclimating myself to their society.

"Indeed. Strata has all the excuses in the universe," says the Highest of the High, "for she carries Kaipor's child."

"Oh," they all cry out. "We must save her *travmeb*, then. We didn't know she was the one."

Myrna, my mother figure, draws me close and bundles me in a soft, white fur. "You have chosen your path then, child. We are pleased."

"My path?" I question, looking about me at all the faces smiling at me so sweetly. "What do you mean?"

Thena, the Highest of the High, laughs softly. Her mirth is like the sound of the purest violin solo. She wraps my heart and floats it calm.

"You have chosen motherhood, Lady Strata. We honor you above all others," she tells me, her arm stretching out around my shoulder, although I've been told never to touch her due to her high position in the Dirzaght world.

I sigh. Motherhood. I had forgotten. I sigh again, then repeat, "Please help me to find my *travmeb*. I am so afraid the Council is torturing him."

Myrna steps close again. "I will take her into the land of Council if it pleases you, Highest of the High."

"We shall all go," Thena answers and her bubble of music is a sweet piano concerto this time. I sway in the music of it.

While I'm enraptured by the sound of its song, all the women gather their furs and food, and we set out into the silvered world of Dirzaght.

The path is not tedious. There is laughter and singing as we walk along. I wonder about being barefoot. My mother used to tell me about picking up ringworm and tetanus if I stepped on something bad, but when I bring it up, the ladies look at me with surprise on their faces. Their eyes hint that they may laugh at me again, but they don't. Instead, they look away as if wanting to study the flowers and trees on each side of the path we're walking.

Myrna, who seems to have adopted me, steps over to my side. Leaning in, she whispers into my ear. "Remember you are Dirzaght. We are immune to all disease."

So Kaipor has told me, I suddenly remember.

We camp out that night. Dinner is stick-poked dough roasting over the fire. No meat. The Dirzaght are vegetarians, but the toasted bread, filled with fruits, nuts, and kernels of grain, is even tastier than before. We smear the paste on the top, which I think is curdled milk but fruit sweetened.

Again for dessert, I'm offered the horrid-tasting green stuff, but this time Myrna insists I eat it.

"For the baby," she tells me.

When Thena gives me a look that says, do as Myrna says, I comply. I suppose the weed thing is rather flavorless, but the color of it is enough to make my face turn as green as the dessert. I follow it up with several generous gulps of water from the communal gourd, which gets passed continuously around the circle of women.

The night is not that cold, but our coats wrap us in just the right temperature for each of our needs. I miss the octopus pillow from the night before, but using my arm as a pillow works well. The crackling fire, the stars shining down, and the companionship of others all bedded down near me send me to sleep faster than any sleeping pill would have.

In the morning, everyone rises quietly and then creeps into the woods for their individual moments of privacy. A wipe is given to me when it is my turn. I'm delighted to see that it decomposes a moment after it's used. When I return to the group, water and soap are passed around. The wash-up is followed by a piece of the bread left over from the night before. The gourd that circulates in their hand-to-hand distribution holds juice.

All the women take two sips, then pass the gourd to the next in the circle. I think of Zoey and how she would have emptied the gourd. There is none of that here. The High Ones are all polite.

It is while I'm waiting for a second turn at the juice when I notice how everyone looks unsmudged and unwrinkled despite their night sleeping in the dirt. I glance down at the pastel blue gown I'm still wearing. It looks much the way it did the day before. How is that possible? I start to ask, but the Highest of High is already calling us to go forward. I fold myself into the herd without pause.

In the afternoon, we come to the Great Lake of Sherman. I step in, and the water tickles my bare feet. I do not go any further. I've had little chance in my life to learn the skill of swimming. Are those in Dirzaght experienced with such things? Even if that is so, it seems too far for them to swim across its width, and I see no boats.

I decide to check, hoping my query won't be viewed as another stupid question from the Dirzaght/Terran neophyte. "How are we going to get across this?" I ask, pulling my toes from the icy lake water.

Like I half suspected would happen, the group's expression collapses into an entire choir of laughter.

"We shall walk across it, my dear," one woman tells me. I think her name is Bana, but she's almost the twin of another called Crissa. I don't dare address either by name for fear of mixing them up.

Tossing her hair back over her shoulder, the youngest of them, Fring, begins to run, gliding over the lake's surface.

I enjoy watching her. She's swan-like graceful, similar to viewing a *Skate on Ice Spectacular.* I expect Fring at any moment to do spins, jumps, and spirals. All she needs is a short skirt and sequins.

Another splits off from the group. I have no idea what her name is. She never speaks to me, or from what I can tell, to anyone.

Myrna comes up from behind me to stand at my side. "Her name is Pyra," Myrna tells me. "She will become your friend in time."

Pyra is as skilled as the other two ladies. She's such a smooth figure skater; in fact, I expect her to perform one of those movements where she spins like a cork, with her leg outstretched, then pulled in to spin faster. I saw it on TV once. I wondered how the skater could avoid getting dizzy.

But I don't understand how they're doing this. The water here isn't frozen. My toe sank down to the pebbly sand beneath it. No special qualities allow for such skating rink expertise.

Two more women set foot across the lake, each with grace and beauty. None of them is sinking as they glide across the lake. The lake is not shallow water, either. The depth of it must be over their heads. But they're on top of it, so I guess how deep a body of water is doesn't matter. Not if you're not plunging downwards.

But I'm not like them. My toe proved that. I sink. I guess being half Earthling robs me of such aptitude. I remind Myrna of that, warning her that I will slip inside the currents of the water and drown if they try to get me to journey over water.

Myrna takes me into her arms to give me a hug. "You have sacrificed much for your people. Do you think we would let you drown, dear Strata? Come. We will teach you the ways."

With her hand in mine, I take a step closer to the lake. Myrna urges me forward. My feet grow wet and cold as winter, but I do not sink. Instead, like the youngest, I slide along, almost floating across the top of the water.

Miracles. Is there no end to them on Dirzaght?

We travel that way for the rest of the day and into the night, gathering close only when bread and water are passed between us. I worry about toilets, but no one seems to feel the need. Nor do we rest. Although I wonder why I'm not exhausted, fatigue is not an issue.

The stars light our way. They speak to us, urging us forward. I have never spoken with stars before. They ring bells for words. Their vibration comforts me. I smile all that night.

When we come to the end of the water, the grassy plains beyond seem to stretch into the horizon, an immense ocean of green. We run through that, our feet gathering energy from the soft pad of our gallop.

At noon, we stop and gather around. We nibble on protein wafers and the same whole grain bread. A gourd of juice passes its way among our ranks. Each takes their two sips, and the jug continues its journey among us. When we are done, we stand and greet the seven moons. Then, we race across the grasslands toward the Council of Men.

That night we perch in the Cluster trees to find our sleep. We climb high into the clouds where the air sings us a lullaby, and the clouds pad our slumber. I ponder on how little food we have eaten and how little sleep I've partaken of, yet I feel more alive than ever. I snuggle among the women, our bodies nesting against each other. The sweetness of our shared dreams scents the air. Again, I wake up smiling.

In the morning, we gallop on, not stopping except at a small creek where we quench our thirst and bathe our travel-worn bodies. At noon, we reach the land of the men.

The Highest of the High knocks at the Council doors. She demands our entry. The great ashen doors of the Council open, and we are welcomed in. A great feast is being spread for us, and all the ladies are matched with men — all of them except me. I sit alone on the throne where they place me. I shed a tear for the empty chair beside me.

"She weeps," one man cries out. And they gather around me, touching my face, tasting the drops that have fallen.

"You bear our future, Lady Strata. Why do you cry?" the men call out.

"You have taken my *travmeb*, and I miss him. Why won't you let him go?"

"Your *travmeb*? You mean Kaipor?"

They stare at each other, exchanging looks of amazement. "Kaipor? We don't have your *travmeb*. The Leoreons do."

I don't understand that, and my tears start up again. In a moment, I am sobbing so hard I cannot hear their speech.

"Lady Strata. Quiet, child. You must not cry anymore. We will find your Kaipor," Myrna promises.

Days go by, and still, I hear no word. I do not understand. Who are the Leoreons? Why have they stolen Kaipor?"

At the evening meal, one day, I demand to be taken to the Leoreons. The Highest of the High rises slowly. Her eyes are scolding me. They have turned gray as a pumice stone. Her voice when she speaks is no longer sweet, but discordant as an untuned string. She lifts her hand and points to me. "You will be sent back to Earth, child, if you reproach us again. We honor you, but we cannot give into your childish wishes. It is not safe."

Then, the oldest of the Council of Men takes me aside. He bids me to sit on a bench in the garden. Then he tells me a story as the Highest of the High looks on, her eyes at moments full of pity, yet at other times, cold as a frozen rock.

"You were chosen, child," the old one begins, "long before your birth was initiated. It was a great honor that fate offered you — this chance to watch the progress of another planet as it grows and, hopefully, ripens into maturity.

You have pleased us these many years with your eyes and ears, with the stories you've told us, with the fragments of knowledge your mind has shared. It was enough. We asked no more of you, but then you came back to us of your own free will — you and your *travmeb* — and you selected an additional path. You have honored us all with the great courage of such a decision."

So far, the old one has told me nothing that I don't already know. I grow anxious for him to get to the point, to tell me why Kaipor has been taken, but I am learning patience from my days with the High Ones. I fold my hands, lower my eyes, and wait.

At last, he reaches the end of his speech, and still, I am no further in my understanding. Yet, I thank him for his story, bow to the Highest of the High, and return to my room. Then as it has happened every night since I arrived in the Council of the Men, tears take me into sleep.

Chapter Two

While I wait for news of Kaipor, I am given a guide named Crismond. He is supposed to calm me and to help me learn the wisdom of the Dirzaght. With his presence, I am permitted to frequent the Council's Hall of Research. It supplements the things that Crismond tells me.

Of course, the first thing I look for is information about the Leoreons. When Crismond finds me a text, I read that Leoreons are a supposedly wise race, although a secretive and very private one. Crismond has told me the Leoreons were angered by Kaipor's action. To rescue me, he disguised himself as one of them.

I vaguely remember the alien image I saw, the one that caused Clarence to toss me aside. It was a dinosaur, a triceratops, I'd thought at the time, but it was not. It was a Leoreon. And their planet has my Kaipor in their prison, where he undoubtedly pays a dreadful price for his choice of illusion.

"But why did Kaipor choose that particular image?" I ask Crismond. The wise one does not know the answer until he looks inside my mind.

"Ah," he tells me then. "Kaipor would have used the Prezvaght transformation, but you feared that species too greatly. So he hunted for another that would not frighten you so. He chose the Leoreons because they were familiar to you. Apparently, something similar existed in Earth's earlier times."

"But, if it was forbidden for Kaipor to take on the Leoreon form . . .?"

"He loves you, child. Of course, he would do whatever was best for you."

I spend my days wandering through the Council's Hall of Research, reading their books, researching the Leoreons, but I am restless.

Several times, Myrna comes to spend time with me, for the High Ones have remained with the men, lending their pleas to the voices of the Council. Myrna tells me she is worried about me and asks if I'm eating enough. Then she wants to know if I am walking in the sunshine and taking in the beauty of the gardens. I try to do both, but everywhere I look, I am reminded of Kaipor. I miss him dreadfully.

Each time Myrna visits me, I beg her to let me go to the Leoreons so I can plead my own case, but the Council will not allow that. I have pleaded with the Highest of the High, but she only smiles sadly or wags her warning finger when I become too vocal. Either way, she negates my wishes. No bubbles of music float up into the sky. Neither one of us can laugh any longer.

Then, one day, the very one who brought me to the High Ones pops into my room. "Why are you still here?" Carthian asks with the same soft voice as before.

"Kaipor isn't in Dirzaght. He is with the Leoreons, and the Council will not allow me to journey there and plead for Kaipor's freedom."

"Rubbish. Why not?" he asks, his forehead clenching with frustration.

Carthian looks all about us as if checking to see if anyone is watching. He sends Crismond off to find some sauna berries for us to snack on. Crismond's absence means that I'm unusually alone for a moment. I explain that to Carthian, and his face lights with a grin so wide it spreads his dimples almost to his ears.

He rubs the bottom of his soles on the carpet and offers me his hand. "Will you go with me again if I take you to Kaipor?" he asks.

I do not even ask how. I nod my head, ignoring the long ago scolding that the Highest of the High gave me for trusting so easily. I would go with anyone who offered to take me to Kaipor.

Thus, I journey from the Dirzaght toward the Great Zomblah, where the Leoreons reside. The night sky guides us on our ziglas, the great beasts who flap their wings and croon soft melodies as they carry us through vibrantly purple sky vistas.

Carthian points out markers, but all the stars look the same to me, and, besides, I am much too excited to listen. I do not learn much from Carthian's instruction, but he doesn't seem to mind. He laughs gently and tickles me under the chin whenever my ziglas' flight passes me close to his.

When we arrive at last, we alight inside the palace as easily as a tired helium balloon gives up flight. The moment we dismount, the ziglas take off, right through the window through which they'd entered.

The inside of the palace is plated in stones, each one boulder sized. The window through which the Ziglas flew is shiny with black obsidian that has formed vertical spears three inches apart. If the Ziglas had missed . . . I shudder to think of how painful that would have been. I'm glad our pilots were so precise in their landing.

Carthian and I are just getting our feet accustomed to the ground again when seven guards rush in and surround us, their tri-prong horns in attack mode. If you can imagine the great size of a triceratops, it gives a fair picture of how big the room we are standing in is.

Carthian calls out, his voice low and full of grumbles and grunts. Apparently, Carthian can speak their language fluently. Always a good thing when lizards the size of airplanes are glaring at you with weapons bigger than a Dirzaght (or a Terran.) The Leoreon guards lower their horns and step back.

I trust Carthian completely, and now even more so. I'm not surprised when we are given permission to proceed.

Unfortunately, it is not so easy to be invited into the inner courts. We wait on the outside of the door that bars us from the Grand Hall, hoping for an invitation to speak to the Supreme Congress. I pace across the flooring of burnished stones smoothed shiny by dragon fire. My Dirzaght friend, Carthian, tells me stories about such things in order to pass the hours of our wait.

Night falls quickly in Great Zomblah. The crystalline panels in the walls that once filtered in light are dulling. The seatless chamber in front of the huge cherry wood doors that prevent our entry grow dim and gloomy. My bottom hurts, unused to sitting on hard stone flooring.

The others waiting for an audience are leaving through the great vaulted doors, heading home, I presume. Perhaps they'll return the next day and the days after if it takes that long. I stand up and begin pacing again as the petitioners trickle out. When the last of them are gone, and only Carthian and I remain, I feel despondent. There has been no word about when the Supreme Congress will let me speak with them. Or if.

At last, my patience is defeated. We have eaten nothing for hours. My throat is parched. I feel drained. Tears of frustration creep down my cheeks. I'm too tired to wipe them away. I let them fall on my gown. They leave dark stains on the fabric's light peach coloring. It would matter to me if I thought I'd be seeing Kaipor.

My temper flares. I can't be patient any longer. I am ready to stride forward and demand entrance. I suggest such a thing to Carthian, but he wags his finger at me and shakes his head. *Never trumpet rage,* he says, *especially not when one is asking for a favor, my dear.*

"But they won't let us in!" I sob. "They refuse to even hear us!"

I don't know how Carthian would have replied to that, for at that instant, the great door swings open, and a Leoreon comes walking out, his tail swishing back and forth as if my presence is a vast intrusion to his peace.

"Where is Kaipor?" I cry out before Carthian can silence me.

The Leoreon bellows harshly, then uses one of his pointed horns to push me back against a wall. *Why have you come here,* he asks. *You are Dirzaght,* I think.

He examines Carthian and then turns back to me. He lowers his sharp horn from its point on my chest, then backs away slowly to examine me more closely.

"Now I remember. It was reported that you were waiting here. You are not from the Dirzaght Council. We checked."

"You stole my *travmeb*. I want him freed. I've come to plead with you."

The Leoreon sits down on his haunches, his legs sticking forward, his tail to the side. He continues to study me.

She must be very young. Her words are youthful. It is obvious that he's talking to Carthian, not me, yet I understand his thoughts.

Did I choose my outpouring wrongly? Perhaps Carthian was wise to advise me that I should be bowing and aspiring to humility rather than challenging the Leoreons.

"Yes, she is a youngling," Carthian says, lowering his head. "Her impatience makes her brazen. She has not yet learned the Dirzaght ways."

She does not smell of Dirzaght. Nor, I think, does she bear the color of your race. Why is that?

"She is a traveler-child."

I watch the two of them, not sure if I should speak. Carthian, as if hearing my thought, shakes his head.

That explains it, says the Leoreon, eyeing me strangely.

Traveler-child, what do you have to give to us in exchange for the embarrassment your travmeb has brought us? Leoreon asks.

I don't know what to answer. I stare at him. "What do you want?" I ask. "Please, can I just see Kaipor first?"

The Leoreon turns back to Carthian. Perhaps they speak without my hearing. They are silent for several moments, staring at each other.

All right. I will take you to him, but he is in our prison, you know.

His soul searching eyes rake my body. I feel faint, but I won't give in to it. I need to see my *travmeb*. I just have to.

The Council has told me that you carry the future. It is not good for you to remain too long in such a condition.

"If it's not good for me, I'm sure it's not good for Kaipor either," I tell him.

The Leoreon laughs. Then, he directs his questions to Carthian. *Why have you brought this stubborn travel-child to us? What business is it of yours?*

Carthian clears his throat. "I like the pair of them. They are both young, it is true, but perhaps they deserve better than this. Kaipor risked much to save his *travmeb*. He knew he endangered his own well-being, but still, he did what he felt needed to be done. His intentions were good. Is that not worthy of mercy?"

Ummmm, the Leoreon says. *I shall ponder it. Follow me.*

We walk down the stairs of many floors. My legs grow tired. The muscles ache, but I continue on. Only when I begin limping because my legs are cramping, do the males take notice.

Then the Leoreon exclaims. *Ah, travel-child. Why did you not say something? Come, I will carry you the rest of the way.*

I am unsure about doing that, but Carthian nods his head and lifts me up onto the Leoreon's back. I wiggle a bit until I can find a place where it is not too rough for my bottom. That is not easy, with the spine-like protrusions sticking up on his back. Still, although it is not comfortable, it is better than the leg cramps. I thank the Leoreon and tell him I hope I am not too heavy.

He laughs. *You are welcome, but you need not worry. You are no weightier than a fallen leaf.*

There are four or five more levels, each longer and deeper than the prior ones. The smell of the walls carries a musty, unused odor. Not bad, exactly. At least it is not damp like most dungeons are supposed to be.

I hear no sounds other than the footsteps of the two males. Perhaps the Leoreons hold no other prisoners. I'm grateful there are no screams or yells for freedom issuing from the passages we pass. But if Kaipor is the only prisoner, why did they bury him in the deepest cells of the prison? Wouldn't his care be easier, closer to the top?

At last I think I feel his presence. The faint odor of eucalyptus teases my nostrils, but I am unsure whether I imagine it or am finally picking up his scent. My body's rhythm speeds up. My lungs breathe deeply, hoping to catch hold of his essence. And I want to scream out,

"I'm here, my love. I'm here."

And then we pass through a long twist in the stone-heavy corridor, and I see him.

He stands up when he hears the advent of our approach, a book in hand, one he was obviously reading.

He doesn't see me on the back of the Leoreon. He merely bows his head, showing his willingness to listen to what the huge Leoreon wishes to say.

But I can't wait. "Kaipor! I am here," I cry out.

He gently sets the book on a table, one with a tall pile of books, papers, and writing materials. He looks up then, searching for me. His face looks mystified, disbelieving.

"I hear you, Strata, but where are you?"

His eyes linger on Carthian, probing him as if the Dirzaght might be hiding me.

"I feel you, my sweetness. But how can this be? You haven't come here, I hope."

"Your *travmeb* has journeyed across the stars. She has argued with the Highest of the High, badgered the Council with her entreaties, and now she pleads with the Leoreons for your release. She has proven well her love for you." Carthian informs Kaipor.

Meanwhile, the Leoreon has responded to my pleading and lowers himself down so I can climb off. I run then toward Kaipor, but Carthian grabs me as I pass him. Holding me against his body, he restrains me. *Easy, Lady Strata. You must listen*, he says.

But I do not want to. I long to reach Kaipor's arms, to feel his lips on mine, to touch him and be held.

The walls are invisible, child, Carthian tells me. *You would hurt yourself if you ran into them.* He takes my hand and brings it to the barrier. I can feel the invisible wall.

"No! Please! I want to go to Kaipor. I need to . . ."

Perhaps it is my tears or the sadness in Kaipor's eyes, but the barrier grows visible and then disappears. Carthian checks that it is safe then frees me.

I rush to Kaipor's side. Our lips meet, our fingers touch. We hug and kiss and speak lovers' words. It is only for a moment.

Too quickly, the Leoreon calls out, *Come back now. It is time to return.*

You must not argue with the Leoreons, my darling girl. Obey me on this. Do you hear me? Kaipor says, shaking me gently until I release my arms from around his neck.

"But when will I see you again? I can't bear this. Please, let me stay with you. Please."

Do not argue, Strata. You must do as you are told, Kaipor says. *I never want to see you imprisoned. You have spent too much of your life at that Institute enclosed by such walls.*

He leads me over to Carthian, who takes my hand. I am too shell-shocked by the shortness of our visit and the way Kaipor hands me to another to say anything more. I am dying inside, torn into tiny pieces.

"Treat her well. She bears our child," Kaipor entreats the two males. Then, he pivots and returns to his cell.

The Leoreon nods gravely. I sense that, but I do not watch. Despite the wounds I now carry from so quickly being severed from Kaipor, my eyes examine every part of him, searching for anything new, anything different.

He hasn't lost weight. I see no bruises unless they are found under his clothing. Was he whipped or beaten by the Leoreons? His carriage is normal, not bowed low like someone who has been tortured or mistreated.

His clothing looks new, unraveled by time. His hair is longer but not unkempt. The Dirzaght never grow beards, so his face is as handsome as ever. What does being in a Leoreon prison mean? Is he okay?

The Dirzaght Council has told us she carries a child, the Leoreon says. *We shall treat her with honor and care for her needs.*

I am not willing to go, to leave Kaipor behind. Is it possible that all this effort was for one tiny minute? But I do not fight Carthian's hold on me, although my tears flow like a summer waterfall, dripping softly.

"Thank you for allowing us this, Carthian," Kaipor calls out. "You are a good friend. Take her back now. There is nothing she can do here."

When I am free, Strata, I will return to your side.

"I love you," I call out to my *travmeb* and watch as the wall solidifies once more, then turns clear and shimmery.

Carthian again lifts me up onto the Leoreon. I do not speak. I am limp from emotion. I know that I can't complain. The Leoreon was kind to let me see Kaipor, yet I couldn't help sobbing on the way up the long series of stairways.

When we arrive at our destination, the Leoreon lowers down so I can dismount. He says that I am to spend the night inside the chamber they have prepared for me. He orders me to sleep well and turns to walk away.

Carthian, too, is to be given a chamber. He calls back, *Be of ease, Lady Strata. In the end, all will work out.*

Inside the room, I find a large pad on the floor with blankets on top. Beside it is a table with a small platter of fruits and nuts. There is a pitcher of water, as well. In the corner, I find a toilet fixture and, beside it, a bowl of water and some soap.

I use the chamber pot and nibble at the food. The night is long, but I find comfort in the fact that I am finally near Kaipor again. We are separated, it is true, but the air I breathe has his breath in it. If I close my eyes, I can almost feel his touch, smell his scent, feel his presence. I think those thoughts, but once again, tears send me to sleep. Will my eyes never stop their weeping?

When I wake in the morning, I see that someone has placed a book on the table. I pick it up and look at it. I am pleased to see that it is written in Dirzaght. Then I chuckle as I read the title: *A Tome of Research on the Planet Earth.*

Because it is very early in the morning, I snuggle back onto the floor bed and begin to read, giggling because the facts the author has written are completely absurd.

Chapter Three

A while later, just as I'm reading about how humans are using technology to grow pouches in their abdomens due to their subconscious desire to become marsupials, a bang on my door announces a visitor.

I have slept in my dress, having no other clothes to change into, so I don't need to grab a robe or anything to cover up. The door opens when I call out *enter,* and beyond my wildest hope, I see Kaipor standing there with his arms spread open, ready to hug me.

"They freed you?" I cry out. "Oh, Kaipor! This is marvelous!"

Of course, I start crying again, but Kaipor grabs me up and carries me back to the floor bed. He soon reassures me that all is well. The richness of our pleasure brings us both a glow of happiness.

Afterward, we talk, and he relates his experiences. I tell him where I've been, and we laugh and kiss and play again. Later, Kaipor shows me how to use the technology of the Leoreons. I'm able to choose underthings, a clean dress, and new shoes. Kaipor does so, too, although his clothes were fresh that morning.

"For a jail," he says, "it was really most impressive. I had my own shower, library, and food and clothing machines. I wanted for nothing except freedom and you."

That brings me back to his arms again, and once more, we fall back on the bed. We're just getting into a deeper level of passion when a voice in our heads says: *Your presence is desired in the Meeting Chamber. Both of you.*

We spring up and restore our clothing. I quickly untangle my hair and braid it. Then we make our way through the elaborate halls of the Leoreons, following a kind of "yellow brick road," in pink, which shows us our way to the Chief Meeting Chamber.

We discover that as long as we go in the correct direction, the guide is a softly muted pink, but if we stray off it, it turns orange. Mischievously, we both have the urge to play a bit, but we don't. When going to Judgment, being naughty is not wise.

As I was saying, the path steers us to our destination, and we arrive at the same cherry wood door where Carthian and I waited before. It opens the moment we touch it. We glance at each other, smile, and swallow some of our anxiety, then proceed on in.

An immense chamber spreads out, as big as a sports arena. The ceiling overhead must be close to three stories high. A giraffe would be humbled. The walls veer up like we're standing beside skyscrapers. It makes me feel very small.

Eleven Leoreons stand facing us. Although each one of them has a heavy horn, sharply pointed with skin-piercing ability, none of them lowers this weapon of choice for an attack.

As we head toward them, they move apart, spreading out to allow us a view of the dais where two more Leoreons stand waiting.

Do I bow or curtsey? I ask Kaipor.

Neither, but be aware they can hear our mind speech perfectly, Kaipor warns me.

We are both silent then, as we walk hesitantly closer. Leoreons are much larger than humans or the Dirzaght. It is overwhelming to be surrounded by so many of them. Yet, I keep remembering the things I read on Dirzaght. Leoreons are friendly. They are wise. They are peaceful, and not prone to step on small humans. I swallow and take several shaky breaths.

Yes, do not fear us, little Dirzaght/human mother. We wish only to meet you and admire your bravery.

I'm not feeling very brave at that moment, but I thank them for the compliment. Kaipor drops my hand and places his arm around my shoulder. Thus, he draws me closer. I want to purr at his touch. I sigh into him, melding my body with his.

We have waited patiently throughout your couplings. We ask now that you hold off a while so we can talk, the second one says.

Couplings? My face burns. How did they know? I want to ask, but Kaipor touches his finger to my lips. Since our conversations have so far been mental and not of the lips, the gesture seems silly, but I understand and comply.

My travmeb is frightened, Kaipor tells them. *I am only offering her reassurance with my body movements. Humans do not bond in public.*

Good! We wish to discuss your prison term. You were sentenced to three revolutions. You have not completed even one, but the tears of the small mother have forced us to override that sentence. There are many who argue against her need. We have debated throughout the night. Yet, humans are fragile. Some of them even give up their lives due to undo stress. We would not wish that. We see no alternative but to return you to her side. What do you offer us in exchange?

They are flying their thoughts almost faster than I can follow. I wish I dared to ask them to slow down, but when things are going well, it's better to remain silent. Besides, I do understand some of it — enough to know that they are freeing my Kaipor.

I have thought on this while I read of your culture, Kaipor says. *I was in the wrong to take your image, yet I erred from ignorance and from great need. I believe my punishment should be to write about the Leoreons and to learn all that I can about your culture.*

While Kaipor speaks, I start thinking about how it would be better if he wrote about Earth since the volume I found by my bed was so ridiculously wrong it was a comedy act.

I wrote that book, one of Leoreons says, pushing his way forward. *How dare you criticize my scholarly work, you CHILD!*

I hadn't meant to send out my thoughts. I still have almost no control over that. Once more, my face heats with embarrassment.

A comedy act, did you say? Another Leoreon from the group surrounding us steps forward. *You found his work to be ridiculous?*

How could that be? That is our most esteemed research on your planet. Does that mean it was incorrect? says another.

I nod, glancing at Kaipor to see if he's upset with me for the interruption, but he's smiling. He darts a kiss onto the top of my nose.

Why, you're brilliant, darling. Of course, it makes more sense to write about the place I live. I shall be happy to provide an additional resource for the Leoreons if that is desired, Kaipor says, most diplomatically.

And so, despite the frowns of the author of *A Tome of Research on the Planet Earth*, it is decided that Kaipor's punishment will be an extensive analysis of what makes humans "tick."

With that settled, Kaipor and I are invited to a great banquet where we are toasted and gloriously entertained by a hoopla-hooping Leoreon named Sharnee, with whom the others appear to be enchanted. (Kaipor is not, though, so I am content to watch her.)

Carthian has already left us. I never got the chance to say goodbye or to thank him for all he did for us. When I mention that to Kaipor, he laughs. *How could he not know your gratefulness, my Strata? You project every thought.*

That hurts, but I shrug. Will I get better someday? It's, unfortunately, not a skill I use much on Earth.

I love you just the way you are, my travmeb, Kaipor says.

Consoled, I move on to my next question. "But who is Carthian? Why did he help us?"

Kaipor plops a piece of kubo fruit into my mouth. "He is a Peaceful, Strata. His career choice takes him from place to place, soothing problems, helping people, and restoring the peace and calm of happiness. He uses a small technological device called a Ripple to locate scenes of disruption."

My mouth drops open. Kaipor shoves in another piece of fruit. I chew and swallow. Then I pour out still more questions, curious about everything. I'm still quizzing Kaipor when, a few days later, we say our goodbyes to the Leoreons and return to Earth.

Returning once again to my bedroom at the Institute, Kaipor does something technical to the time continuum, so we arrive more or less at the same time as I left with Carthian. That means we can make good use of our night together, and we do. Delightfully.

In the morning, when I wake, it's a normal day. I'm glad. I'm exhausted from traveling around the galaxy. I want nothing more than to slip quietly into my reading or to work on a story. However, life never flows based on one's needs and desires.

Dr. Schmidt walks into my room before I've even risen from the bed.

"Dr. Schmidt!" I cry out, happy to see that he's returned to the Institute.

"You gave us a real worry," he says, sitting down in a chair beside me. "I had to come back to see if you were all right. I was concerned, Child. Too many things have happened to you and around you, chiefly because you stir them up."

I shrug. I'm sure he's correct, but I didn't cause Tom's murder, and I certainly didn't force Clarence to take me to the cemetery with him.

"You don't have to be anxious, though, about Clarence anymore. He won't be returning to the Institute. He's been taken into custody, and . . ."

"He's alive?"

I forgot to mention that, darling, Kaipor interrupts. *As much as I wanted to gore him with my horns, as a peacekeeper, a member of the Dackor, I really cannot be violent.*

I'm so glad, Kaipor. I never want you to hurt anyone, my love, not ever!

The love term is enough to perk Kaipor up. He sits down on the bed and smiles at me.

"Why did you think Clarence was dead, Clea?" Dr. Schmidt asks. "Did you believe you'd killed him? Or was it the aliens who came . . .?"

"Kaipor saved me, Doctor. I thought he'd killed Clarence. That's all."

Dr. Schmidt frowns. "John told me that you were doing better. He spoke highly of your recovery. Do you still see aliens, Clea?"

I laugh. If only Dr. Schmidt knew where I'd just been — seeing Leoreons and the Dirzaght on planets trillions of miles from Earth, but I don't bother to explain. I just nod my head. Let him think I'm crazy. Maybe I am.

"There are no aliens, Clea. Repeat it. NO ALIENS," Dr. Schmidt tells me.

I peek at Kaipor. He's lying on his back, staring up at the ceiling, and he's laughing so hard he's vibrating the bed. Of course, Dr. Schmidt doesn't see that. He wouldn't notice if the bed got up and flew across the room. Humans never take notice of what they've resolved not to see.

"Dr. Schmidt, you can make me state that a hundred times, but I doubt that it will have any effect on the alien child I carry inside me."

"What?" Dr. Schmidt jerks his head up. "What are you talking about, Clea? Are you pregnant? Whose child is it? Was it from the time Joe tried to rape you? No, the doctor said you were still a . . . Did Joe come back again, Clea? Or has someone else touched you?"

Was it wise to tell the humans this, my love? You could have waited several months before they suspected. With fat clothes, maybe even longer.

But I'm proud of it, Kaipor. I want everyone to know I'm carrying your child.

I am happy you feel that way, but I shall have to inform the Council of your action, Strata. I do not know how they will accept it.

"Did Joe come back again, Clea? Or has he or someone else forced you to do what you didn't want to do?"

I shake my head. Both males have overlooked the important part. I'm going to be a parent, and I must plan for it.

"Are you sure about this, Clea? When did it happen?" the psychiatrist asks. Without waiting for a response, he stands and lifts up my hand so he can take my pulse. Then he checks my heartbeat through the stethoscope hanging down from his neck. That done, he inhales, holds it, and wipes his forehead with the back of his hand.

He's not sweating. It's just an old habit of his, something he uses to relieve pressure, a precursor, I've noticed, to when he's developing a bad headache.

"It will be okay," I reassure Dr. Schmidt. I'm only . . ." I pause, trying to calculate.

Five weeks, seven days, Kaipor supplies. *However, the gestation of a Dirzaght is nine and ½ months, slightly longer than a human's.*

I relay that information to Dr. Schmidt, but he only looks at me and shakes his head. "Poor Clea," he says. "You had made such great strides forward. I was hoping . . ." He doesn't finish the thought, but I know. He was hoping that I'd get out of the Institute and live a normal life. I have to chuckle at that. My life could never be normal.

Because of the psychiatrist's visit, I've missed breakfast, so before Dr. Schmidt leaves, he calls the kitchen to send up a meal. Then, he makes an appointment with the new medical doctor so I can be checked over.

That's why at 9:30, I go downstairs to the clinic. I've been there only a few times, although never because I was sick. The Dirzaght are never ill. At least, that's what Kaipor always tells me.

I relay that information to the new doctor, but he doesn't seem impressed. He ignores my words and does the exact same things that Dr. Schmidt did earlier. He takes my pulse, checks my blood pressure, and, just to be cautious, verifies my temperature. Then, he wants me to stand on the scale. I'm five foot four inches tall and always weigh the same 113 pounds.

"This is silly," I tell him. "None of these tests will determine if I'm pregnant or not."

Be patient, Kaipor scolds me. *Do not rattle the humans. Let things proceed on their own course now.*

I know he's right, so I sigh and say nothing when the doctor hits my knee with a sharp, little hammer. I kick up at him instinctively and then laugh at the silliness of it.

"So," the doctor says. "How long have you gone without a period?"

"I've never had one," I tell him.

The doctor, a new one since the Institute runs through medics like it does aides, which is about one for every three months, checks my files.

"Ah, I see," he says. "Why do you think that is? You're not obviously unhealthy in any other way. You don't engage in competitive sports. You're of an age when menstruation should be regular. What have your previous doctors said about it?"

I laugh. So far, this is actually quite fun. "When I tell them that Dirzaght females have given up menstruation, they simply accept that and move on to their next question."

"I see," the doctor says, and he glances at Dr. Schmidt, who has just entered. "Why is this girl not under a medical doctor's therapy? She should be menstruating at her age. We need to do some blood tests and give her a thorough physical."

"She has already been through every test," Dr. Schmidt says, sighing. "There seems to be nothing physically wrong with her. She appears to be in perfect health. Just give her a pregnancy test, please. That's all I asked you to do."

Dr. Kroager's face glooms over. His eyebrows descend down into his eyes, and he looks like he's about to argue the point with Dr. Schmidt. But then I see him reconsider as if he suddenly remembers that Dr. Schmidt is the big cheese of the Institute. The new doctor clamps his teeth together, turns to gather up his charts and papers, and says, "All right. Clea, you may undress in that room over there."

I follow the direction of his pointer finger and make my way into a cubby-like room where one of those doctor's office examination beds is lined with white tissue paper. A blue-flowered paper gown sits on top of it. I start disrobing. They've turned the air-conditioner on for some reason. My skin turns into jumping goosebumps. Kaipor's warm arms are all that keep my teeth from chattering.

You know what he's going to do? I remind Kaipor. *They did it after Joe tried to rape me. The doctor . . .*

I know, Kaipor says, cutting me off. *It is primitive. I could tell them what they want to know,* he says, laying his hand on my stomach. *The child is growing well. It has no problems. But you will have to go along with it now, Strata. You started this, remember?*

Kaipor's assurances would never stop the approaching exam, even if my *travmeb* were allowed to materialize and explain the situation. So I sigh, smooth out my crinkly, flowered gown, shiver, and try not to think about what's about to happen.

About ten minutes later, the doctor, accompanied by one of the Institute's newer nurses, enters the room. "Are you cold?" the jerk asks.

When I nod, he makes an effort to reassure me, "This won't take more than a minute," he says, and then he proceeds to wash his hands, slip on the white plastic gloves, and take another peek at my chart. Meanwhile, the nurse has me lie back on the paper-covered bed and place my feet into two ice-cold metal stirrups. I feel like I've been turned into an upside-down frog waiting for the scientists to dissect me.

The clock on the wall clicks teasingly. I try to hold my breath, counting the ticks that pass, wondering when the doctor will start his probe. When I get to eighty-five, he steps over to the "observation deck" and asks, "You okay, Clea?"

I want to snap at him, but Kaipor shakes his head at me, so I only sigh again and nod. It is completely unfair that our current medical examination procedure is so much like rape. As a rational patient, I must lie there, silently condoning/accepting what this stranger is about to do to me while he performs an act so intimate my whole body blushes from the invasion. Without even an apology, the man's finger invades, probing deeper than Kaipor's ever has. A tear drops from the side of my eye.

"It's almost over," the nurse tells me, patting my arm.

"Not quite," the doctor disagrees. "I'm going to go ahead and give her a pap smear. Since she's obviously sexually active, we need to take some tests for other things, too. We'll check her blood for sexually transmitted diseases.

"Why haven't you been using protection, young lady? Aren't you aware of the dangers?" he asks me.

I start to inform Dr. Kroager about how the Dirzaght don't have human diseases, but I know he won't listen. So, I close my eyes and wish I were anywhere else. Unfortunately, the doctor's not through with his physical and verbal abuse. He removes his finger and sticks a metal probe deep inside me. "I'm just doing a little scrape here," Dr. Kroager tells me. "Have you had multiple partners or just one, Clea?"

"Only my *travmeb*," I tell him.

"Sorry, I don't keep up with teen jargon. What is a travmeb?" he asks, pausing a moment to stab my insides.

Before I can complain, he removes the instrument and the touch of his hand, and then says that I can sit up. I take my feet out of the stirrups and bolt up. "A *travmeb* is like a husband," I tell him. "At least, I think so."

"Well, if that means your partner is free to visit other girls, you better make sure that you're protected from now on."

I do not visit other females, Kaipor is quick to reassure me.

I smile at Kaipor and send him a mental kiss.

"May I get dressed now?" I ask the doctor. He nods, strips off his gloves, and walks out of the room.

When I'm clothed in my own jeans and blue sweatshirt, the doctor returns to take a sample of my blood. Then, he gives me a container to urinate in. Kaipor frowns about the blood samples but is extremely amused by the urine sample.

He, in fact, offers to supply it for me. I snicker over that, wondering what would happen if the samples were from him. Would his specimen shock the medical world, or would they just say that the urine was contaminated?

The next day, I'm paged to come down to Dr. Schmidt's office. When I arrive, he tells me with a very strained expression that I am definitely about to become a mother. There is no smile on his face. He is not happy. In fact, he looks about as pleased as he would be if the detective, Langston Simons, were to suddenly show up and start asking probing questions again.

However, I'm delighted at the confirmation. I float back up to my room, gloating because I finally have proof that I'm not crazy. An alien who impregnates CANNOT be imaginary!

Chapter Four

The next day, Dr. John takes me outside for a walk. He wants to say goodbye since he's departing to join the staff of another mental hospital. I'm glad that we have a little time together for his leave-taking. I've grown fond of him, even though he never understood about aliens.

At least, sometimes, he tried to believe me, and, after all, belief in things you can't see is something few humans are skilled at, so I'm not overly surprised when he couldn't go beyond a certain point.

Is he competition? Kaipor asks, dropping into my thoughts. I wasn't expecting my *travmeb*. He startles me so much I jump.

"You all right?" Dr John asks.

I nod. I don't tell the doctor what caused me to flinch, of course. I let him think I just stumbled over something on the lawn.

As we walk, Demon, the guard dog, begins to howl. He lives in a large pen at the back of the grounds. Usually, he just sleeps during the day. I've never heard him carry on like he is this time. "Can we go see what's causing Demon to bark?" I ask. "I think something's wrong."

Dr. John stops and stares at me. "You want to see that dog? Why, Clea? Didn't Clarence use Demon to threaten you?"

"That's not the dog's fault. Besides, I think Demon's trying to tell us something. Maybe he's got a paw caught in the fence or is hurt."

The day is beautiful. The flowers we've planted in the front yard are smiling with small flags of color. The birds are singing in two-part harmony. The air smells sweet with the scent of a freshly mowed lawn. I can hear the machine of one of the groundskeepers as he rides the mower around the back acreage, but it's the sound of Demon's frantic bark that calls to me.

"It really does sound like something's wrong," I tell the doctor. "He's never howled like this before. He really needs us."

Dr. John looks at me strangely, but I suppose he's by this time used to my saying and doing odd things, so he just shrugs and allows me to lead the way back into where the Institute's old kennel is located.

Dr. Schmidt once told me there were twelve dogs at one time. The Institute even used to breed them and bring the puppies in for the patients to play with. Those days passed with the danger of lawsuits and allergies. Now, only Demon is kept on the property. It seems a waste with all the available acreage. Most of us would love to have some puppy antics to entertain us.

On the way to the kennel, Dr. John and I pass a couple of barn swallows with beaks full of twigs. I pause a moment to watch their flight. They've started a nest in an overhang. Amazed, I stand and listen for the sound of their babies, but then I realize, of course, they don't have young ones yet. It's only the beginning of spring. Birds are just now building their nests. Even so, their young will hatch before mine does.

True. Our child will remain in your womb longer than a human child, but he will not burden you for as great a period of time. Within a year, he will be ready for small feedings of scholarly learning, Kaipor comments. *Then, by the time he is four, he will pursue advanced studies.*

That is new information for me. I grow silent thinking about it.

Dr. John touches my arm. "Are you worried about the baby?" he asks.

I'm amazed at how intuitive the man is. How did he know that my thoughts had sped from the scene of the nesting birds to thoughts of the child I carry? I smile at him. "I was just listening to Kaipor, Dr. John. He keeps telling me things I don't know. Sometimes, that can be a bit distracting. It's like having a phone conversation with two people at the same time."

Dr. John frowns. "Ah, poor Clea," he says, expressing so much sadness that I want to console him but can't find the words to do so. After all, if he doesn't believe that my reality is true, what words can I offer to explain them?

We walk on, crossing the newly mowed grass. Small bits of the grass collect on our shoes. Dr. John shakes his shoes. He dislikes such imperfections in his appearance. I rather like the delicate little blades of life. I wonder why shoes aren't decorated with such trimmings. Green is such a lovely color.

As we approach Demon's pen, the dog becomes so excited at seeing us that he jumps up repeatedly, throwing himself against the wire enclosure as if we were his best friends.

"What's the matter?" I question him softly, but another step takes me close enough to smell the odor of his surroundings. It's obvious that his pen has not been cleaned for several days.

"Phew!" Dr. John says as he pulls out a handkerchief and uses it to cover his nose. "His pen was never dirty like this before. I wonder what's going on?"

"He doesn't have any food or water, either. I bet no one has given him any attention since Clarence was jailed."

Dr. John looks as upset as I am. He pulls out his cell phone and connects to the control room of the Institute. Immediately, he starts giving someone "what for." I take a step closer to the fence.

"Hi, there, Demon," I say cautiously, half-prepared for a nasty reaction. But the dog doesn't seem angry with me. Instead, he acts desirous of my attention.

He won't hurt you, Kaipor assures me. *Dirzaght can communicate effectively with most Earth animals. I shall teach you how.*

Is there anything you can't do? I ask, teasing him.

All that I am I shall share with you, my darling. You are my travmeb.

Then show me, Kaipor. I want to learn. You can start with Demon. How do I speak to him? What do I say? How can I become his friend?

Kaipor gently grasps my head between his palms. His eyes stare into mine. *Listen,* he says.

I hear the sound of a locomotive barreling down a wooden trestle and the wind sweeping up autumn leaves. A waterfall splashes, tumbling down into its pool. Tree limbs creak on a blustery day. The voices of a wolf pack howling at the moon echo across the hills.

The resonance of all of it filters around me and inside me. It rushes through my blood and into the veins inside my arms, flooding my body with the sounds of nature. Suddenly, I understand. In that moment I can see and hear and feel the call of everything around me.

Good, my love. Well done, Kaipor says as his hands drop, and he steps back.

I am stunned by the changes in me. For a moment, I want to cling to Kaipor's hands. I have an impulse to throw myself at him and kiss him in gratitude, but I do not.

Instead, I glance back at Dr. John. Seeing that he's still engaged in his lengthy conversation, I walk toward the pen's gate. The lock slips off the moment I touch it. I open its door and call out softly to the formerly vicious dog. Ecstatic, Demon barrels out of his pen, rushing toward me.

Dr. John explodes when he sees Demon out. "What were you thinking?" he yells at me, but the dog is so happy he's dancing in circles around me.

"Heel," I order, remembering the word that Clarence used. The dog circles once at my side and then sits.

"Good dog," I tell him, patting his head.

Dr. John takes a step toward me, but the dog's ears flatten, and he growls at the doctor.

"Behave," I command, and the dog swings his head back to look at me. He licks my hand and rubs his muzzle on my jeans.

"Good boy," I tell him as I pat his head. His tail flaps back and forth, hitting my leg with sharp thumps.

"Come away from him," Dr. John orders. "He's a guard dog, Clea. You can't trust him. He's supposed to drive patients back inside, not kiss their hands. I don't understand this."

Demon starts to growl again when Dr. John speaks. I correct the dog sharply, and once again, he licks my hand.

The doctor takes a step closer, but then Demon jumps sideways and makes a dash for him. I call out, ordering the dog back, but Dr. John starts running, and the dog nips at his heels.

So much for dog training, I tell Kaipor, and he laughs.

Come, walk with me. We never have the chance. Let's do it — just the two of us, he says.

I take Kaipor's hand, and we head for the wooded area back behind the Institute property. A blue jay sweeps down to give us a scolding welcome.

Kaipor trills to it, and it alights on his raised finger.

"He's so beautiful," I say, breathless with wonder.

Talk to him, Strata.

I say "jay jay" a couple of times, and the bird tilts his head and stares at me, but he doesn't get as friendly with me as with Kaipor.

Do it again, my travmeb urges, and so I try, but the bird only flies off, expressing his disgust at whatever I've just said.

Kaipor chuckles. *You're adorable, you know.*

Then he scoops me up into his arms and carries me deep into the woods. The trees are so thick that it's dark inside their midst. The sunshine is a filtered medium of shadows. Kaipor sets me down in front of a giant oak tree. Then, he takes out a pocket knife and begins to cut into the wood.

"What are you doing?" I ask as I try to stop him.

He glances down at me. *You must not interfere in this, Strata. It is an old Earth custom I've read about.*

I can't stop Kaipor from doing anything. He knows that, but he watches me a moment to see if I'll argue. I shrug and mosey over to a nearby boulder. I plop down on it and sit there watching him, petting Demon, who's just rejoined us.

Despite the fact that I can't see the sun, it does heat the air, and my face feels gloriously alive from the warmth. "I wish people could gather energy from the sun," I tell Kaipor.

And stop eating? He says, chuckling as he carves.

I see what he's doing then. He's stripped away a heart-shaped area of bark. His hands, as he forms it are sure and steady. I watch as he adds our names and entwines them with three carved ivy leaves.

Strata + Kaipor = Threll

I guess I'm dumb, but I'm thinking that Threll must be an alien word for love or something, so I ask for the definition. Kaipor turns to look at me, and his smile broadens into a laugh. *Ah, my darling. Your innocence is showing again. Threll is the name of our son.*

"Threll? Where did that come from? I was thinking about Eric or John, like the psychiatrist. Besides, maybe it's a girl."

Kaipor pockets his knife and walks over. *Our child is a boy, Strata.* He studies me for a moment. *John, huh — like the psychiatrist who was just walking alone with you? I do have competition. I shall not accept that at all, my fair lady."*

Kaipor grabs me up and tosses me into the air. I scream, of course, but his hold on me as I come down is secure and even tighter than before. And the kiss he gives me as his lips lower . . .

"Clea!" we hear as someone makes his way toward us. Then, another and another approach, all calling my name.

"I'm here," I yell, wishing I didn't have to. Kaipor smiles and sets me down. *Our tree is there. We have achieved our purpose,* he says, whispering into my ear. Then he fades out, and I can tell by the absence inside my mind that he's really left.

Demon has started barking again. In fact, he's carrying on like a mad dog. It takes all my efforts to keep him from charging the approaching search party. But with my hand on his collar, I hold him firmly at my side, though his lunges are fierce, and his fur is ruffled up like a yowling cat's.

"Clea!" Dr. Schmidt shouts out. He is the first to spot me. "What on Earth are you thinking? Were you running away from us?"

I shake my head. My whole body is concentrated on holding onto Demon, and it's harder than before because, apparently, Dr. Schmidt is not on Demon's list of friends.

"Carlos, take the dog," Dr. Schmidt calls out, and one of the aides strides forward. Demon doesn't pay him the slightest bit of attention. All his anger seems focused on the doctor. Carlos makes a grab and wrestles the dog away from my grasp. Demon, realizing what has just happened, whimpers like a kicked puppy.

Then, Dr. John comes up to me. He takes my shoulders in his hands and turns me to face him. "You have not acted like an adult, Clea. I shall be speaking to Dr. Schmidt about taking away your privileges for the week. I am certain you will not be seeing a movie this Friday."

"Why?" I question. "I didn't run away. Besides, I'm not an adult, Dr. John. You've told me that often. I'm still only a teenager, well, at least sometimes," I say, thinking about the freedoms that supposedly came with my eighteenth birthday.

Dr. John's face hardens. "Don't be impudent, young lady."

I don't mean to be. I glance at Dr. Schmidt, but his eyes are not looking at me. He's staring at the oak tree.

"Do you have a knife, Clea?" Dr. Schmidt demands. Then, without waiting for an answer, he pulls me up against his body and does a swift search. He finds nothing. "Where is the knife, Clea? Where did you put it? How did you get a blade to scar the tree like that?"

I shake my head. "I don't have one. I've never had one. Kaipor did that," I say, pointing to the tree. "He just told me that our son's name is going to be Threll. I don't know if I like that name or not. Don't you think it's kind of odd?"

"That is enough about aliens, Clea. You're going back to the Institute right this minute, and for the next week, just as Dr. John has requested, you are deprived of all your freedoms."

The two psychiatrists share a look, one that tells me not to bother arguing. They're both at their point of overflow. I guess the mystery of the carved tree has maxed them out.

"You're going to be a parent soon, Clea. Whether you like that or not, it's time that you stop these fantasies and become an adult," Dr. John admonishes me.

As the two march me back to my home, I pass by Demon. His tail wags and he whines dreadfully, but I'm not permitted to stop and pet him.

"Ouoo," I say to the dog as I walk on by, and his tail beats a faster rhythm. "Ouoo," he answers back.

Chapter Five

I have so far been avoiding writing my French essay about Napoleon Bonaparte and his fascination with conquering other nations. I dislike the whole subject. War is archaic. I think people wanting to engage in any kind of battle are demonstrating weak personalities and emotional immaturity. But, despite my personal opinion, there remains the assignment: a three-paged essay on my opinion as to whether, in the long run, Napoleon Bonaparte was beneficial or not to France.

Ack! Well, at least, being grounded in my room allows me the time I need to get down to the business of it. Sighing mournfully, I begin my research. It's easy with Internet access. The first thing I find is another student's already written essay. Of course, it's not in French, and its subject is a little different than mine.

Peter Chau's essay is just a historical analysis, and he talks about how Bonaparte was good for the nations he conquered. I read his essay and discover that it's possible the French "emperor" was actually not a bad dictator. Sure, he was egomaniacal and tyrannical, but he was also benevolent in some ways. He improved the structure and framework of every government he conquered.

That's all very interesting, but it doesn't actually help me with my French essay. I move on, studying the monarch's maxims, a word which I have to look up. (I find out that it means a truth or general principle.) An example, one that I don't like, is the following: *A man like me troubles himself little about a million men.* That, I think, is the quote of a mad man, and it reconfirms my original viewpoint of him.

Grating my teeth, I read on. Napoleon thought that women were only useful as "breeding machines?" Urgh. The man suddenly falls into my hate list, especially when I read that he discarded his first wife for political convenience.

However, mandated school projects rarely allow for freedom of choice, so I continue reading despite my dislike for the things France's esteemed leader said.

I do find several maxims I can approve of. Bonaparte wrote: *Different subjects and different affairs are arranged in my head as in a cupboard. When I wish to interrupt one train of thought, I shut that drawer and open another. Do I wish to sleep, I simply close all the drawers, and then I am — asleep.*

I really like that quote. I can almost see Bonaparte, relate to him, understand what makes him tick. That passage makes him seem almost human to me.

Humans are like cupboards? Kaipor interjects, dropping into my thoughts.

I turn to look at him, but I can't see him.

"Don't do that," I scold. "Either show yourself or don't pop in at all. I was working on my schoolwork, you know."

Sorry, my love, he apologizes, coating his body with image, head-first and then downward.

"Thanks," I say, feeling like a bully for being so dictatorial. "It's not that humans are like cupboards, exactly," I explain to make up for being snappish. "It's that I understand what Napoleon was saying in that quote.

"You see, we do focus on something, and in doing so, we close the drawers of others. It's like our thoughts stand in line at attention, waiting for us to accept them in, and if we choose, we can push them all aside, shutting the cupboard door, so to speak."

Kaipor laughs. *I love such illustrations. They are so enlightening to my understanding of the human character.*

"Don't the Dirzaght do the same thing?" I ask, blushing because I realize that I am removing myself again with my phraseology. "I mean, don't we?"

Kaipor ignores the slip of the tongue. *A Dirzaght can handle many brain wave channels at the same time. Our thought processes blend notions and ideas together and then organize them according to priority so that none are ignored. Remember the female dance team you saw on television, how they weaved themselves together so that two lines became one? Dirzaght can handle multiple streams, integrating them all into one while pushing the priority items to the front.*

I think about it for a moment. Isn't that what humans do, as well? It's why brain sorting keeps us awake at times. Perhaps we're not as fluid with it as the Dirzaght.

I glance back at Napoleon's maxim, studying it again. I really like how he put it, but I'm not sure how easy closing cupboards is at night. Sometimes, at least for me, the drawers keep popping open. Sometimes, they invade my dreams.

"Do Dirzaght dream at night?"

Of course, Strata. We solve most of our problems during sleep. That is more efficient than attempting to do so while awake. We simply lay the jumble of our thoughts out like cookies on a cookie sheet, and in the morning, they march in rows more simply — all equations neat and ordered, the colors and flavors blending deliciously.

I giggle. I doubt they even have cookie sheets on Dirzaght, but I love Kaipor's imagery. I stand up and walk into his open arms. For a moment, we blend in a kind of lovers' sweetness.

Later, after Kaipor flits away again, I return to dig into my search for the real Napoleon. I still have the question of my essay to solve. Did the French leader develop his country in a productive manner?

I read about the wars he fought. He conquered Italy in 1796. He whipped four generals in Austria. He beat the Turks to take over Egypt. Then he battled and battled again and again, building up more and more territory until his defeat in 1812.

War is the business of barbarians, he once wrote, yet he spent his life fighting. How confusing.

Still, I have to concede when my analysis is done that Bonaparte did pick up a chaotic nation and force it back onto the right path. It was true, he veneered a layer of good atop his conqueror's role. So, in spite of the fact that Bonaparte wanted to take over the world and declare himself the monarch of everywhere, I have to admit in my essay that he did assist France with reforms that encouraged equality and fairness.

Besides, anyone, in my opinion, who abolished serfdom and the Spanish Inquisition, which tortured and maimed all the people who were dragged before it, couldn't be a hundred percent bad. I liked the way Bonaparte established a national bank and attempted to develop a free and equal education for everyone (except females.) He essentially tried to protect the common man, and that's a good thing.

Having the general idea then of what I want to say, I begin to write. French is not an easy language for me, but it is a beautiful one. My fingers weave the story of a man who has many egotistical problems but still paves the way for growth in France and, in the end, brings enlightenment and a freer society for all.

I am just putting the finishing touches on my French essay when Rupert knocks on my door. When I call out for him to enter, he opens the door and says, "You're wanted downstairs."

"I'm not allowed to leave my room," I tell him, not looking up since I've just seen a spelling error on my report.

"Yeah? Well, it's Dr. Schmidt who ordered you to come."

"Why? What does he want?"

Rupert shrugs, then adds, "You've got a visitor."

I sigh, put my essay down, and stand up. My back is stiff from sitting so long, cramped over the computer. I feel old because of it. I bend over and touch the floor, then laugh as my back pops itself into position.

Rupert isn't amused. He taps his foot and says, "You coming? I've got things to do in the men's quad. A new patient's arriving in an hour, and I have to clear out Tom's stuff."

"You mean his personal effects are still there?" I ask, using the terminology I'm gathering for my mystery novel. I see from the expression on Rubert's face that he thinks that's a stupid question, but he comments anyway. "The police finally released it. We couldn't move anything before."

On the way down, Rupert doesn't talk. I start wondering if Dr. Schmidt will be in the visitor's room, too, ready to give me another lecture. The day before was when the psychiatrists thought I tried to escape.

How silly they are — as if I'd want to leave the Institute. Someday, I will, I know. Someday, I plan to go away to college, but not yet. The Prezvaght still prowl. They would find me if I left now. They would haunt my nights and my days with their slathering teeth and their carnivorous ways.

The Prezvaght will not hurt you, Kaipor whispers into my ear.

Remember? You are one of us.

I ignore him. Kaipor's smart, but he doesn't know everything. The Prezvaght are all around me. They watch me always. Maybe they wouldn't kill me, but they would kill my friends. They'd destroy my life, somehow.

Rupert leads me to the visitor's room, where Langston Simons is waiting. The detective stands when he sees me and walks forward, his hand outstretched to shake mine. I look around, surprised because I don't see Dr. Schmidt.

"Why are you here?" I demand. "I solved your crime. What else do you want from me?"

Detective Simons drops his hand. I'm glad he doesn't insist on a handshake. I have no patience today, not for fakeness. Napoleon Bonaparte once said, *Men are moved by two levers only: fear and self-interest.* Which lever is it that moves Detective Simons?

"You and I have business to conduct," he says.

I have no idea what he's talking about. I did his job. I solved the mystery. Why should there be anything else to connect us now?

Apparently, he can read my blank look. He smiles. "There was an award for Tom's murder, Clea. The Society for Clarity offers it for people who strive to assist the police in such matters. They've given me a check made out to you for five thousand dollars."

I laugh. "What would I do with that?" I don't extend my hand to accept the check any more than I offer my hand to him to shake.

Detective Simons' eyes darken in puzzlement. "What's wrong with you, Clea? Why this sudden coldness?"

How can I explain? I try to swallow back the disgust I feel when I remember how Detective Simons let me down. It was Kaipor who saved me, the alien that no one believes in. Where were Detective Simons and the policemen who were supposedly there to bail me out if something backfired? Why did they leave me on my own? Why did they turn their backs on me?

I drop down into a chair and pretend I didn't hear the detective's question. I wonder why Dr. Schmidt let me out of my room to talk with Detective Simons. It's obvious that permission was given. Does the psychiatrist know about the check? Are they all in cohorts against me?

"You're not talking to me?" the detective asks, coming over to sit down on the arm of my chair.

I start to stand up, to move away, but he reaches out his hand to stop me. "Clea, tell me. What's wrong?"

I sit back to avoid his touch. Then I look up at him. "You would have let Clarence rape me. You would have let him kill me. He was going to, but Kaipor saved me."

"Kaipor? You mean one of your aliens?"

I nod. Detective Simons shakes his head. "Clea, we had that place surrounded within minutes of your arrival there. The only thing stopping us from seizing Clarence was you. I wouldn't let anyone risk you getting hurt."

I stare at him. He looks earnest. "But I didn't see you. I didn't see anyone except Kaipor."

"Of course, you didn't see us, Clea. But we were there. When Clarence dropped you, it was because the groundskeeper called out. Except it wasn't a groundskeeper. It was me."

"No one called out," I argue with him. "Kaipor disguised himself as a Leoreon, and Clarence got scared. That's why he dropped me. He thought he was going to have to fight a Leoreon."

Detective Simons laughs nervously. I can tell that he's thinking I'm crazy.

"I have no idea what a Leoreon is, Clea," he says, "but I sure didn't see one. Now you take this money and put it into your account," he orders as he pushes the check into my hand. "Then one day, when you're doing better, you'll have it for college. I imagine it will help with tuition, or at least pay for your books and some of those other fees . . ."

The detective stands and takes a step back. Suddenly, I see myself through his eyes.

"You didn't see anything strange?" I ask. "You didn't see a dinosaur-like creature standing at the top of the stairs when Clarence tried to carry me into the mausoleum?"

"No," Detective Simons answers, shaking his head and looking so sad it's as if he's one blink away from tears. "An officer had a dog whistle. He used that to call Demon. Then, after we got the dog out of the way . . ."

I interrupt the explanation, trying to piece it all together. "But what made Clarence drop me? What scared him so badly?"

"I don't know the answer to that, Clea. We didn't mean for him to drop you — not like that, anyway. I'm sorry he hurt you. You hit your head pretty bad. Did it give you a concussion?"

"No," I say softly, confused once again. I want to explain to Detective Simons how I traveled to Dirzaght hunting for Kaipor and then to Leoreon to rescue him, but I know Mr. Simons won't believe me.

I close my eyes and think. I was so sure about everything. The memories were so vivid, but did the trip really happen, or is this just another proof that I'm crazy?

"I'm sorry, Clea. I have to go now," Detective Simons says. "I have business in town. I just wanted to drop this off for you. You were a big help, you know. Take care of yourself, Clea."

I watch the detective walk away. Then I call for Kaipor, but he doesn't hear me. I'm alone.

As the door closes, I realize the Prezvaght have come. They're all around me, drooling, sharp-toothed, red-eyed with glares of hatred. I scream.

Dr. Schmidt is the first to arrive. He comes for me and takes me back to my room.

"Am I crazy?" I keep asking him, but he doesn't answer me. Instead, he gives me a shot and tells me to lie down on the bed.

I hand him the check. I have no use for it, not if I'm crazy. What does an insane person need with money, after all? I ask him about that, too, but he only soothes me with the same sounds my mother used to use long ago before the Prezvaght turned her into meatloaf.

"I can't face it if there aren't any aliens," I tell the doctor. "I can't bear not to have the Dirzaght."

"I know, Clea," Dr. Schmidt whispers. "Don't think about it right now. Just relax. Let the tranquilizer calm you. It's okay. The detective's gone. We won't let him come back again, Clea. Not if he disturbs you like this."

"He said there weren't any aliens. He said he rescued me and that it wasn't Kaipor who did so. But I flew to Dirzaght. I got Kaipor out of a dungeon. How could I be wrong? I couldn't make that all up. It's not possible."

"You have to relax now, Clea. Think of the baby."

I sit up then. "The baby? How could I have a baby inside me if there's no alien? Answer that, Dr. Schmidt."

"I don't know, Clea. Only you can tell us who the father is. For now, anyway. When the baby comes, we can run a test on it. Then we'll know."

"A test? What kind of test?" I scream, fighting against the doctor's hands on my arms.

Rupert steps forward, taking my left hand. "Easy, Clea," he says. "It's going to be okay in a minute."

But it won't be. What are they going to do to the baby? What tests? They'll find out that it's alien. They'll know I wasn't lying then, but they'll take my baby. What will they do to him?

"Threll. He's to be called Threll," I tell them.

"Yes, Clea. You told us," Dr. Schmidt says.

The warmth of the drug begins to float me across the skies. I'm flying without gravity. I close my eyes and see the stars from Dirzaght.

"Don't you see them?" I ask. "The stars are different. We're on Dirzaght now."

"Yes, Clea. Close your eyes and look at the stars. They're very beautiful, aren't they?"

I nod my head. "Beautiful."

"Sleep, Clea. When you wake, it will be okay again," Dr. Schmidt tells me.

I sigh. I feel tickly warm all over. My body is swollen with good feelings. I smile and give in to them.

When I wake, Diana, one of the newer aides, brings me food. I breathe in the different whiffs of potential flavor. They all smell delicious.

"What did you bring me?" I ask as she removes the cover.

"They have given you cream of chicken soup, a piece of bread, and some chocolate pudding. How does that sound?"

Sounds horrible, Kaipor says.

"Where were you?" I yell out.

"Easy, Clea," Diana says. "Do you need the doctor?"

I sit up. "No, I'm fine. Just leave the food, please. I don't need you to feed me."

Diana screws up her face, which makes her appear even uglier than usual. She looks like a man. She even has a small hint of a mustache. I know she's as strong as Rupert. I look away from her face to avoid losing my appetite.

"I'm not going anywhere," Diana says, her voice a deep baritone. She slides her chair back a little and crosses her arms. She reminds me of a prison guard.

Kaipor has been strangely silent. I look over at him. He's semi-visible. I can see through him, but his outline is evident.

Why didn't you come when I called you? I ask.

I went back to Dirzaght. I told you that I needed to inform them about the humans finding out that you carry our son.

"Eat," says the aide, and her cheek ripples with something that looks like anger

I pick up my spoon and attempt to sip at the soup, but it's still hot. I blow for a second and then slide the first spoonful in. Diana sits back against the chair. Her eyes close, but I know she's listening.

What happens to our son when he's born? What if the humans try to take him from me? I ask.

That will not be allowed. Threll will be removed if they attempt that.

I drop my spoon. Diana's eyes pop open. She glares at me.

"Sorry," I say. "I don't know why I'm so clumsy today. It must be the effects of the medicine they gave me."

Diana grunts and closes her eyes again. "Eat," she says with her deep, gravelly voice.

I pick up the spoon and shovel in another bite. I nibble at the bread, too, but I'm watching Kaipor.

Would you take my son away from me?

Kaipor looks uncomfortable. He stands up and begins pacing. *They may not allow you to keep him here, Strata. In fact, I'm sure the humans won't let you keep him.*

Then let me go with you. Let me live on Dirzaght.

Kaipor turns to look at me. He rushes to my side, picks up my hand, and then, glancing at the snoring guard, he asks, *You would be willing? Would you give up Earth to live on Dirzaght?*

If that's where our son is and where you are. Of course, I would.

Kaipor kisses me. There is great joy in his eyes.

"What are you doing?" Diana demands, lurching up from her chair. Of course, she can't see my *travmeb*.

Kaipor kisses me. There is great joy in his eyes.

"What are you doing?" Diana demands, lurching up from her chair.

I suppose I must look very strange, my arms around an invisible body and my lips pursed for a kiss. Kaipor slides back from me, laughing. I place my tray back in my lap and pick up the spoon. Diana's gray eyes narrow. As if she suspects someone else is in the room, her smallish eyes rove about, inspecting the walls and furniture. But she can't see Kaipor, even though he's across the room making faces at her.

I stifle my laugh and take another bite of soup. Diana's heavy, gorilla face eyes me. Then, she falls back into the chair. It groans. I think for a moment that the chair will give way and land the aide on the floor, but it accommodates her massive girth, its cushion sinking halfway to the ground.

Kaipor blows me another kiss, and I work on finishing my food. The soup is cold. The bread is soggy with slightly stale margarine, but the pudding is dark, rich, and delicious.

Zoey and Melanie come in to see me that evening. "Hey, what's up?" Zoey says, taking a seat on my bed.

Melanie stands there staring at me, nervously rubbing one barefoot against the other.

"Sit down," I tell her. "I'm glad you guys came to visit me. It's been really dull around here unless you count Diana, the gorilla guard."

Melanie giggles, then glances over at the door worriedly. "Are you sure we won't get in trouble for coming here?" she asks Zoey.

Zoey gives Melanie a firm Zoey look, and Melanie sits down on the same chair that Diana occupied earlier. She looks lost in its now permanently lowered cushioned seat.

"Hey, I heard that you're P.G.," Zoey comments, as usual, blurting things out like she's immune to courtesy.

I nod and watch Melanie pick at her sweater. She's collecting the little fuzz balls off it like that's her top-secret mission. She plucks a ball with her left hand, then checks to see if anyone's coming through the door, then bends over the sweater to search for more of them. Her eyes are furtive. Her right hand clutches her wad as if she's collecting gold dust instead of fuzz.

"Melanie, what are you planning to do with that?" I ask as I nod at Zoey, letting her know that her news is correct.

"Who did it?" Zoey asks like we're discussing another murder mystery.

"My *travmeb*, of course," I tell her, irritated that everyone asks me the same question.

"You mean the alien?" she says, wrinkling up her nose. "No, really, Clea. You had to have slept with someone, Clea. Babies don't come from the air, you know."

"Unless it's an immaculate conception," Melanie adds, still attacking her sweater as if collecting fur balls were a matter of life and death.

"Look, you guys. Kaipor is an alien, but he's as manlike as Chris or Rupert."

"Or Joe?" Zoey says, examining my face.

I sigh heavily. "It wasn't Joe, Zoey. My son is Kaipor's."

Melanie looks up and stares at me. For a moment, she forgets about defuzzing her sweater. Her hand falls open, and the clump of fur drops to the ground. "It is the men's habit to rape," she says. "They lie about it. All of them do. But they rape and rape and rape."

Zoey and I look at each other. We don't know how to respond to that.

I have never raped anyone, my love. I would never be violent or take someone without their desiring me.

I know, Kaipor. But Melanie doesn't understand that. She knows only about the bad kind of men.

Would it help her if I brought a Dirzaght here to teach her the joy?

I start laughing. Both Zoey and Melanie turn to stare at me. They, of course, haven't heard my conversation with Kaipor. Melanie looks hurt, thinking I'm making fun of her. She stares down at her hand, realizes the ball of fuzz is gone, and searches for it. When she finds it, she reaches for it and tenderly picks it up.

"It may be handy, you know," she tells me when she sees my eyes following her actions. "My uncle would not like fuzz in his eyes. It would stop him. He would leave."

Zoey and I exchange glances again. I wonder if Melanie has taken her medicine. She's probably pocketed it again. Lately, she's been collecting things: toenail clippings, spoons, pills, and other people's personal items. Last week, they found a collection of rotting peas under her pillow, lying next to three rolls of toilet paper and one of the nurse's lost keys.

"Men think it is their right to take things," Melanie tells us. "But I take things, too. Tonight, I shall take two desserts. Do you think that will be okay?"

We both assure that she can have ours if she wants, but she shakes her head. "No, if you give it to me, that's not the same. Did the alien give you this child?"

It takes a moment for me to switch gears, to comprehend what she's talking about. But then I understand. I see what she means. "Yes, Melanie. When we make love we give to each other. Neither one of us takes. We only give."

Melanie smiles. "That is good, then. I should like a child of my own. May I have yours? Would you give him to me?"

Zoey answers for me. "Melanie, you know she can't do that. Clea is the baby's parent. She's his mother. Mothers don't give their children away. They love them always."

Melanie stabs at several fuzz balls. She reminds me of a penguin I once saw who pecked at the moving reflection of someone's mirror. It grew angry when its beak came up with nothing, but it still pecked and pecked.

"There are good men, Melanie. Kaipor is one of those. He doesn't bring pain and grief."

For a moment, Melanie stops poking at her sweater and looks up at me. "I want an alien, too, then. I will collect aliens."

Kaipor chuckles, but it isn't funny. It is sad. Zoey reaches over and takes my hand. "You deserve this happiness, Clea. Don't let the psychiatrists or anyone else take it from you."

We're having this chat in daylight, yet Julia drops in, apparently overhearing our conversation. "You are discussing men?" she asks. "I do not like them."

"I was just telling Melanie that Kaipor is not like other men. He's kind, and he cares."

"Chris is nice, too," Zoey adds, although she doesn't seem quite as sure about him as she was the last time she mentioned their romance. I'd wanted to ask her how it was going. Now she's given me the opening. But just at the moment, I'm about to ask her, Julia pounces.

"Chris? I remember him. He flirts with the nurses. He's not faithful."

Zoey jumps up off the bed. "What do you mean, not faithful?"

"He's like all men. He plays with hearts. He eats them and spits them out."

"Stop it, Julia. Chris isn't like that," I say, defending him for Zoey's sake.

He loves her, Kaipor adds.

"See, did you hear that? Kaipor says that Chris loves Zoey," I tell the ghost.

Julia's face grows icy. She glares at me as she slides off into the wall. We all shiver from the coldness she's left behind. Her anger has left a residue of arctic winter.

I throw a blanket over Melanie's shoulders and then turn and hug Zoey who's started to cry.

"Don't listen to Julia," I tell her. "She's warped by what happened to her."

"I heard that," Julia says, floating back into the room. "Have you ever felt a ghost ram through your body? It makes a mortal ill," she tells me, and then she heads in a beeline toward me.

"Stop!" Kaipor yells out as his body materializes between the ghost and me.

Behind us, Melanie screams. Zoey does, too, but she's apparently thrown a blanket over her head first because her screams sound muted. Julia, stopped by Kaipor's body, measures my *travmeb* with her eyes, glowers at me, then suddenly winks out.

Chapter Six

After Julia takes off, there isn't any reason for Kaipor to fade away. After all, my friends have now seen him. So, he sits down on the chair that Melanie gave up so she could cluster with Zoey. Kaipor smiles at the two women and says, "I am very sorry I frightened you. I didn't mean to. I just couldn't allow my *travmeb* to be injured."

I run to him and give him a great big kiss. Then, I thank him for saving me by plopping down in his lap and curling up so I can play with his silvered hair.

Zoey and Melanie, at first, are rather tongue-tied.

"What are you doing here?" is the first question Zoey asks when she gets her tongue working again. "Do you know how much trouble you've gotten Clea into?"

Kaipor sighs. "I am Strata's *travmeb*. Of course, I must be with her. I do not understand how I have caused her trouble."

"Like she talks about aliens all the time, and she has no proof, so they think she's loco?" Zoey shoots off her mouth in her usual blunt and objectionable manner.

"That's not Kaipor's fault," I try to explain.

Zoey's eyes are almost scary because she's so mad. "Yes, it is, Clea. If Kaipor had ever come out of hiding, he'd clear you from all that, then no one would think you belonged in this loony bin."

"But then they'd take him away," Melanie says suddenly, causing us to stare at her. She feels our amazement and thinks we're disagreeing with her. "They would, you know. They'd run tests on him. They'd kill him, too."

"They couldn't. Kaipor would just disappear again," I reassure her. "Like Julia, he can slip away at a moment's notice." I kiss him again because I'm proud of his ability. Not all Dirzaght are as skilled as he is.

"Yeah, and when they said they'd torture you, he'd come running and slip right into their traps. That's what kind of happened here, isn't it?" Zoey adds.

I sit up. "You're smarter than that, Kaipor, aren't you?"

"I would give my life for you, Strata. You know that," he tells me, taking advantage of the proximity of my lips.

"You don't look human," Melanie adds out of the blue.

"Why should he?" Zoey laughs. "He's from that place Clea always talks about… Drizzle?"

"Dirzaght," both Kaipor and I say at the same time.

"I like that suit you're wearing, though," Melanie says. "Is that the fashion on Dirzaght?"

"For males," I tell her. "The women wear the most beautiful flowing gowns. I had one, but I had to give it up. It doesn't belong on Earth."

"What was it like there?" Melanie asks, sitting up straighter. "Could you sketch it?"

I notice, then, that Melanie hasn't been picking at her fuzz balls. Her hands are loose and unfisted. Her mouth isn't twisted with fear anymore.

I shake my head. "It's impossible to describe, Melanie. We don't have the colors that they have on Dirzaght. It's like the swirls of ice cream when you're just beginning to stir. The colors ripple. Even when you walk, you see different shades."

"How beautiful," Melanie says. "I wish I could go there. Do you think I could?"

"Kaipor?"

"The Council would have to . . ."

"You'll ask them? Will you really?" I interrupt to coat his face with a hundred kisses.

"Easy, my love," he chuckles. "You forget that they say, 'no' the moment they see me coming. I'm not the best diplomat for your requests."

"Would they say 'yes' to me?"

His eyes smile into mine. "How could they not? One smile from you and Earth's moon would crawl into your hand. The sun would shine forever if you asked it, the . . ."

"All right," Zoey breaks in. "We get the message. So the Council likes Clea, or is it Streta?"

"Strata," Kaipor corrects her. "That is her Dirzaght name."

"I repeat. Is it the Council that's so enraptured with our friend here, or just you?"

I giggle because Zoey is always so very Zoey.

Kaipor gives me a look; then he, too, breaks into chuckles. "All right, Zoey. You're correct. I adore her, but the Council does honor her. She grows our future inside her."

"What do you mean?" Melanie asks. "The baby?"

"Our son is to be . . ." Kaipor glances down at me and then closes his mouth. "I cannot discuss this. It is forbidden."

"Whoa," Zoey says. "What do you mean forbidden? What are they going to do with Clea's, I mean, Strata's child?"

"It will not be harmed, of course," Kaipor reassures us all. "Our son will be revered. It is just that this is not something we can discuss at this time. It is not allowed."

"Will he be alien or human?" Melanie asks.

"He is who he is," Kaipor says. "Now I must go. They come."

I don't know how he does it. One moment I'm sitting in his lap, and then I'm suddenly on the bed with Zoey and Melanie, sitting up straight, pointed in the direction of the door.

Someone knocks, and without waiting for my permission, the door opens, and Dr. Schmidt is standing there staring in at us.

"Why are you here?" he demands gruffly.

Melanie springs up. Her fists scrunch, and she searches for fuzz balls. Zoey doesn't move. She looks the psychiatrist in the eye and says, "Why shouldn't we be? We're Clea's friends."

Dr. Schmidt looks surprised by the argument. It's like he's never thought about his patients having friends. He stares at each of us for a moment, considering, then says, "Oh, I guess that's all right, then. I just stopped to see if you were feeling better, Clea. Are you?"

I nod. I'm too amazed for words. Things have been happening too quickly to keep up the polite dance. I swallow and attempt to say something, but it's not needed. Dr. Schmidt gives a brief bow of his head and retreats, closing the door softly.

"Oh, my God!" Melanie says, and she turns and stares at us.

Zoey cracks up and throws a pillow at her. I throw one at Zoey, and before we know it, we're all giggling and silly. Then, since Kaipor doesn't reappear, Melanie brings the conversation back to the fashions of Dirzaght, and I have to tell her everything I can remember.

Finally, with her persistence, I get out some plain, white computer paper, and Melanie, with my descriptions, begins drawing the gowns of Dirzaght.

Melanie is an artist. She draws unbelievably accurate pictures of the dresses I wore on Dirzaght. Then she sketches several others I tell her about having seen among the High Ones. Even without color, the dresses seem to ripple with changing lights. Melanie has shown the delicate luminosity of the material just by her pencil shadings and by the folds she places in the gowns. The dresses, themselves aren't exact, but they're close enough. I'm positive that Kaipor would recognize them as Dirzaght.

After she completes the last sketch, Melanie leaves to go back to her own room so she can transfer her drawings into her art book, where she keeps all the fashions she's drawn. She tells me that she's going to apply colored chalk to blend in the rainbow hues I've told her about. She wants to show how the dresses swirl and dance with various tones until you're really not sure which color to call it. I can't wait to see the final drawings.

Zoey, bored with the whole thing, took off long before Melanie finally finished. With Kaipor still gone, Melanie's departure leaves me alone.

Immediately, I open up my writing site. I have several e-mails, as usual, but I ignore them (not my usual mode of action since I normally can't wait to see what people have said about my stories). But this time, I don't want to get sidetracked. I make a beeline for my favorite forum, Captain Colossal's. That is the three-hundred-word flash fiction contest that I often enter. I've been too busy lately to participate, but with no one around, I'm determined to try my hand at the day's contest. I scroll down to the posting: Today's prompt: Write a story that takes place near a railroad track.

A railroad track? What do I know about trains? I've never even ridden one. I've never been anywhere near train tracks. That means that I can't do an adventure story. My ignorance would show up in the story. This tale will have to be either science fiction or fantasy.

Aliens? Should I have a flying saucer land on the railroad tracks? Maybe they'd confuse the tracks for a human? No, that's stupid. Aliens would know that railroad tracks are dangerous. They'd avoid them, figuring that a train might be coming.

So, a fantasy? Should I write about fairies? Unicorns? I certainly don't want either fairies or unicorns getting hit by a big, old black locomotive chugging down the tracks.

What else is fantasy, I ask myself? Then I have it — a dwarf, like the kind in Snow White and the Seven Dwarfs. They live underground, I'm pretty sure. At least, they do in most stories. Dwarfs are miners, aren't they, after all? So this dwarf could pop out of the ground and suddenly see a train coming. I think about that a while, not really liking the story yet, but feeling the fuzzy shape of it. The story is like a far-off house concealed from staring eyes by a thick, damp fog. I need some sunshine to clear away the mists.

Sometimes, when I'm just starting to draft a story, I prefer to start out using good old-fashioned pencil and paper. Then I jot down my thoughts: the dwarf, the train, the tracks, and his wrinkled old face. That stirs up my brain. It defogs the story. I scribble a few words, then stop to chew on the side of my pencil.

First, I have to name my dwarf. I want a funny name, but would a dwarf, a serious, self-confident dwarf, put up with a silly name? I shake my head. My teeth carve impressions on my number two-leaded pencil.

Then it comes to me — Peabody. I have no idea why, but I like the name. It seems funny for a dwarf, but still possible. Peabody. I draw a picture of the train tracks standing next to him. But a dwarf, if he lives under the ground, must dwell inside of mountains. He's come out of a hill, I suppose, and I pencil that in. Then I start to type:

Peabody the Dwarf and the Mighty Train

The dwarf wiggled his nose as he crawled up out of the hole at the side of a hill. Something was different. He sniffed deeply and looked all about him. Somewhere in the vicinity, the stench of metal alerted him to mankind's presence.

Peabody sat down in a patch of grass and scratched at his head. He'd come this way only a couple of centuries ago. It just didn't make sense that humankind would have reached this deserted area.

Suddenly, the dwarf bolted up. The ground was rumbling. The air was filling with smoke. Peabody eyed the top of the hill. Something was coming.

The dwarf's short legs climbed him up the side of a rocky bluff. When he reached the top, he saw two snail trails of steam and a huge, ugly, smoke-breathing THING coming at him. Peabody darted to the side, slid down over the top, and tumbled the rest of the way until he landed in a heap.

He was just in time. The metal monster passed by and rumbled on.

After it was several feet away, Peabody stood up, clutched his fist in the air, and yelled, "Ack, you're nothing but a coward! Come back and fight me!"

The monster continued to growl, but it was obviously fleeing, chugging faster and faster over its double metal slime trail.

The dwarf shook his head, sighed with relief, and wiped at the sweat fear dripping down his forehead. He stood another moment, bravely but fearfully, watching the horizon for any signs of the monster's return.

Then, satisfied, Peabody limped back into his hole, closed the hard-earth door, and scurried down the tunnel. He could hardly contain his joy as he began weaving a tale about his extreme bravery, a feat that he would soon recite before the entire town council.

The End

Just as I finish typing my silly story, Kaipor pops in and bends over me to kiss my cheek. I smile at him but continue what I'm doing. I still have to post the story in my portfolio and then in the contest. Kaipor, finding out that I've written another story, demands a copy so he can read. I print it out for him, finish up my business, then turn around to look at him.

"Well?" I ask. "What do you think?"

I love you, Strata, he says, *but there are no dwarfs on your planet.*

I laugh. "Don't be silly. Of course, there aren't any. This is fantasy."

Kaipor shakes his head. *Fantasy? No. Some Dwarfs live on Crudon but not in the hills underneath railroad tracks.*

I stare at him a moment, checking to see that he's not teasing me. "I suppose that unicorns and fairies live there, too?" I ask, still unsure whether he's joking.

He looks up from reading and nods his head. *Of course, my dear. With the dragons, the elves, and the flying pigs.*

The twinkle's back in his eyes, so I don't pursue it, but I wonder. What if fantasy really isn't fantasy? What if it's just the reflections from another world?

Chapter Seven

Langston Simons visits the Institute again on the following Monday. I know he does because I'm dragged down and into Dr. Schmidt's office to meet with the detective. That's when I discover that I have to testify against Clarence.

"No," I say at first, shaking my head. "Everyone saw what he did to me. You were there. You watched him kidnap me. I wasn't willing to go with him. He had a grenade and a gun. He didn't give me any choice. He threw me into the car. The dog almost bit me, too, because he wasn't a friend then.

No one stops my babbling, so I continue. "Clarence drove me to the cemetery. I hate cemeteries, do you know that? All those dead people. I thought I was on the route to being dead, too, and would get buried with all the other bones and decaying flesh. I was sure Clarence was going to kill me there and cover me up with dirt.

"You said you saw him dragging me up the mausoleum's steps. I wasn't willing to go with him. You know that, so it was a crime. Everything he did was against the law. He's a criminal. So why do you need me to testify? Didn't others see everything, too? Weren't there cops all around? You said there were. Why do you need me to say anything?"

I've run down, so I stop and pant from my lack of air, but I'm not finished arguing.

"We need a statement from you, Clea," the detective says as coldly as if we were strangers. Obviously, whatever friendship Detective

Simons once pretended, it's dried up and flown away.

I sigh. I'm sitting in the black leather chair. It's not the one that patients use. I feel odd. Langston Simons has taken my chair. I suppose he doesn't know any better. I wonder why Dr. Schmidt didn't explain.

I turn to look at the psychiatrist. "Do I have to do this, Dr. Schmidt? Is it really necessary?"

The doctor has his pipe stuck in his mouth, just like he used to do before he got sick. He swivels his chair around to look into my eyes. Then, he pushes his pipe to the side of his mouth so he can speak. "It would be better for you, I think if you did not, my dear. I believe that too much has happened lately. You've slid back in your progression toward … Well, let's just say that your health has declined a bit."

Dr. Schmidt stops and mouths his pipe for a minute, thinking. My eyes flit to Detective Simons. I check to see if he's angry over Dr. Schmidt's words, but the detective doesn't show if he is. His legs are loosely crossed at the ankles.

He never fidgets like Dr. Schmidt. Detective Simons merely sits and waits. Perhaps his insides have turned to stone. How can a person not show what he's thinking and feeling? What causes such hardness?

Dr. Schmidt removes his pipe so he can talk a bit. That's a sign that he's prepared to lecture. I sink lower in the massive chair and wonder where Kaipor has gone this time. I dread hearing my psychiatrist say something I don't want to hear.

"However," Dr. Schmidt continues, "sometimes, we must do things that are not good for us individually. We must serve the greater good, distill the value of our soul, endure the hardships…"

"Doctor, I have to return to the office shortly. Is it possible to speed this up?" Detective Simons interrupts. "Can't you just simply tell Clea that she should go and be done with it?"

My mouth flaps open and closed before I can stop it. I'd never dare say something like that to Dr. Schmidt. How can Detective Simons? How can a police detective be so brazenly rude? Where does he get the confidence?

This is juicy, Kaipor inserts, sitting down on the arm of my chair. *The human power struggle is ever so fascinating. I see the testosterone flying about like the fur of two fighting cats.*

How would you know about fighting cats? I snap, uncertain whether I'm glad Kaipor's back or irritated because he's returned to interfere again.

Dr. Schmidt, after giving the detective a piercing look of annoyance, continues as if he hadn't been interrupted. "Clarence would have killed you, Clea — at least that's what Langston has told me. That man must be locked up. It is my opinion that we must all do what we can to see that justice is served.

"Remember Tom? If Clarence is truly guilty of that patient's death, then Clarence must be punished. You were instrumental in dragging that up. Would you back away from the case now? Would you allow Clarence to kill someone else?"

That is shallow reasoning, Strata. Go with the detective if you wish, but do not allow the psychiatrist to talk you into something you don't want to do. I think it would be beneficial for you. You would get out of this place, at least. You would be free for a while.

All three men are staring at me. I search the knees of my jeans for reassurance. The knees are faded, as if I've worked too long scrubbing floors, moving about knee-ward. Yet, the pants aren't timeworn. The newest fashion demands a lived-in look, which is why the jeans came from their crinkly, new package all faded and half-washed away, the material soft from its chemically enhanced old age.

"Does a crime always have to linger around month after month?" I ask. "Once it's solved, can't it just go away?"

I suppose that's a stupid question, but I feel like the Clarence/Tom thing should already have wrapped itself into completion. The case was solved after all, the murderer was caught. Why can't it be finished?

That's what I want. I can't bear to think about all the things that could have happened and to continue discussing and discussing it as if it were something recurring daily. I want it to be over.

All the nightmares that keep waking me have finally started to lessen. Instead of the constant horror of Clarence with his hands and arms like octopus tentacles, binding me to a sweaty, fear-reeking body, my dreams have settled down — now they're only about snarling, snapping dogs and the ever-present Prezvaght.

A resolution to this case will help you, Kaipor assures me.

Detective Simons shakes his head and erupts with a loud chuckle. "Crime never stops, Clea. It's a ripple that spreads ever wider."

Nice analogy, Kaipor agrees, nodding his head. *Too bad the guy's competition; I rather like him.*

"He's not competition!" I cry out, forgetting to mind send.

Of course, my words make no sense to the doctor and Detective Simons. They look at each other as if to say, here she goes again.

The detective stands up, sliding himself from the chair as if prepared to dodge should an attacker suddenly dart out from the shadows. "I'd like to get Clea's statement on the books, but if she's not up to it . . ."

"Okay, I'll do it," I accede, checking for Dr. Schmidt's opinion. His eyes give me the approval I'm searching for.

I sigh, pleased that I've done the right thing. I've, at least, made Dr. Schmidt happy.

Detective Simons wants to take me to the precinct that very instant, but I'm not dressed suitably. I ask for five minutes and run up to my room. I discard my jeans and tee, grab a dress, and pull it over my head.

What a shame there's no time to take advantage of such a disrobing, Kaipor tells me, tugging at the skirt as if I need his help to clothe myself.

"Stop it," I snap. "I don't need you to interfere." I slip my feet into the same sandals I was wearing a moment before. Then I turn around and look at him. "I'm sorry, Kaipor. I don't mean that. I'm just nervous. You are coming with me, aren't you?"

He has stepped back, giving me more than adequate space. I can tell from his look that I've injured his feelings.

"Kaipor?" I repeat. I don't really know what I want to say. Why are relationships so complicated? Why doesn't he just know what I need? Isn't that what reading my mind means?

He grins a rather shaky smile, and his eyes soften as he watches me. *Do you really want me to come?* he asks, and I suddenly hear the doubt in his voice, doubt that I've never heard in him before.

"Please," I stand frozen to my spot across the room from him, too astonished by his uncertainty to take the steps forward that would send me into his arms.

Do you find Langston Simons handsome? he demands. His eyes darken, and for a moment, they look more like Prezvaght eyes than Dirzaght.

My thought shatters his jealousy. He walks forward and corrals me with his arms. *No, my travmeb. I could never allow violence to rule me. I am Dirzaght.*

I take in air as best I can. The arms around me are warm and tight, but I don't resist them. I don't even resent their firm hold.

"I'm sorry," I say. "I am filled with fear. It ripples like the circles of crime that Detective Simons spoke of. I know you're not Prezvaght. I know that."

Kaipor holds me for a moment. Then we head down the stairs to find the waiting detective. Only after we see Mr. Simons, do I remember that I haven't reassured Kaipor.

I love you, Kaipor. Detective Simons is only a policeman I know. He means nothing else to me.

Kaipor offers no response. As Detective Simons and I walk out of the Institute, I realize that although I feel my *travmeb's* presence beside me, he is not commenting on everything as he usually does. He is strangely silent.

I'm surprised by our method of transportation. Instead of the police car that we rode in before, we have only a plain and very ordinary junk heap of a car.

"What is this?" I ask, trying to keep the distain from my face and voice.

Detective Simons glances over at me, sees my face, and starts to laugh. "Ah, Clea, I've forgotten how emotive you are. This is my regular car. I do a lot of plain-clothes detective work, you see. Sometimes, I don't want to make an announcement about who I am."

The front seat of the car is old and cracked. The leather is peeling in strips. "This isn't my first choice for transportation," I tell him, hooking myself in with a belt so old I suspect it won't hold me in case we have an accident.

"Don't put the car down, Clea," the detective laughs. "This old carcass has a couple of extra cylinders. It goes from zero to ninety in nothing flat."

I'm holding onto the rickety, old armrest on the passenger door. The thought of going ninety doesn't thrill me a bit.

The windshield has two bullet holes on the side. My pinky might fit through them if I lean forward and test it. I take a peek at the backseat. The cushion in the rear has been patched with duct tape. I can see the sticky leaking out.

I glance down at Detective Simons' shoes, wondering if this is really the same man who always showed up at the Institute in spotless, fashionable, and immaculate clothes. Today, he's wearing a pair of jogging shoes — the generic kind with pasted on emblems, a cheap Chinese copycat. Detective Simons follows my eyes and then nods his head. "This is my alter image, Clea. Sometimes, I have to dress like a slob, other times like someone who shops in Beverly Hills."

The detective starts up the car. It doesn't cough or sputter as I'd thought it would. Instead, it purrs like it's a new engine. I have to admit that if my eyes were closed, I'd think from the sound of the motor that we were in a mint condition car.

Detective Simons is a good driver. He heads out the long, circular driveway as if he were driving an old lady. I hardly feel the car's acceleration as he drives forward or his stop when he arrives at the main road and has to wait for a couple of cars to pass. Then, when he heads out into the road, his foot presses down, but I'm not jolted by it. The car doesn't rattle and thump like Clarence's old Chevy, and I don't bump up and down when it hits rough spots.

The detective grins at me when we've gone a couple of miles. "What do you think now, Clea? It may be ugly, but everything else is the equivalent of my Silver Bimmer."

I have no idea what a "Silver Bimmer" is, but I figure it's some kind of car that he's really fond of. The truth of the matter is that all I know about autos is that you need a license to drive one, and to get a license; you have to pass a battery of tests.

We pass by the Shaara Dairy. It still has cows in its meadow. Zoey told me once that they actually milk their cows by hand and sell the milk to whole food markets. The cows are the old-fashioned black and white ones. As they stand in the shade of a gigantic oak tree, chewing their cuds, I think they look happy. I wish the Institute would buy milk from that dairy. I'm positive it would taste extra special.

"Do pretty cows make better milk?" I ask.

The detective laughs. "You don't get out much, do you?"

I shake my head and see his smile almost immediately drop away as he realizes what he's just said.

"Sorry, Clea," he apologizes, and the car purrs on down the road. For the rest of the trip, we sit in strained silence.

When we arrive at the police station, it feels as if I'm entering a military camp. Identical police cars are all lined up outside in straight, horizontal rows. Everywhere officers are walking about, each wearing matching uniforms in black and white, a gun strapped to their sides as if they expect the enemy to attack at any second.

I hear them calling out to each other using military names: lieutenant, captain, sergeant, major, chief . . . and addressing each other with a sprinkling of "sirs."

As we enter through the heavy doors, I see several policemen with long rifles. I thought those had been exchanged for Taser guns. One officer is putting ammunition into his rifle, just as calmly as if he were loading up one of those small candy toys that comes in the shape of cartoon characters and pops out pellets of sweetness with each shot.

A man at the desk, who wears several stars on his lapel like a general, calls out to Detective Simons. "Hey, Langston. Who you got there? Isn't she a little young for you?"

I blush, but that isn't the worst of it. Kaipor, who's been quiet during the drive, suddenly becomes animated.

How dare he talk about you like that, Kaipor bursts out. Then, before I can say anything, my *travmeb* streaks off toward a nearby desk, picks up a soda can that's sitting there, and carries it over to the sergeant at the entryway.

Kaipor, no! I cry out, but he ignores me. A second later, Kaipor pours the remnants of the soda down the front of the loud-mouthed officer. The man roars like an angry lion, but there's nobody nearby that he can yell at. Of course, neither he nor Detective Simons can see my *travmeb*.

Detective Simons stops and stares at the angry officer. The man is wiping at his shirt as he glances all about, searching for someone to blame. The detective gives me a strange look and shakes his head like he's imagined it all. Then he takes my elbow and walks me forward.

I don't know if Detective Simons noticed the coke floating through the air or saw it pouring itself down the front of the sergeant's shirt. Maybe the detective didn't catch that sight, but it's obvious the cola somehow stained the man's shirt and is currently sitting once more over at the desk by the wall. I wait for Detective Simons' questions, but they never come.

A loudspeaker blares out announcements as we're walking down the hall. It hammers out names and commands as if the ranks were assembled, standing at attention, ready for orders. "Johnson, report to room 7. Curtis, dial 9-4-6. Franklin, call Lieutenant Baymer."

The stern, formal atmosphere of the place is frightening. I swallow hard and follow Detective Simons like a limp puppet. We make our way through a maze of artificial walls and office cubicles until we reach the musty-smelling, dark area toward the back where a door with a dirty rectangular, glass window pane is etched with the words: Langston Simons, Chief Detective.

"Cool," I say as the detective opens the slightly warped door and stands to the side for me to pass into the room.

"Didn't you come here before?" Detective Simons asks.

I shake my head. The last time the detective took me to the station we went into a room at the front of the police station where we were crowded in like a small horde of insects gathering around a rotting fruit. I shudder at the memory. It was not a pleasant experience, although afterward, Detective Simons was kind to me again. That was before he found out about the aliens and before he got scared that Kaipor might be real.

Just like the room we used before, Detective Simons' office has almost nothing in it, only a desk piled high but neatly with manila folders, a plain, beige telephone, and a large computer monitor with a keyboard whose letter names are half rubbed off — oh, and against the other wall, a tannish-brown and dinted file cabinet, the top drawer of which is slightly askew. On the top of it is a shiny coffee mug with a reproduction of the Mona Lisa.

"Not exactly fancy, is it?" I say. "Couldn't you at least buy a nice, green plant?"

Detective Simons glances about as if seeing it through my eyes. "Yeah, just like with the car, elegance gets in the way, Clea. I prefer it without the pictures and the plants. The more personal the room, the more the criminal finds out about you."

"But it's so hard on you not to have anything to bring you back to who you are," I try to explain.

"Sit down, Clea. We're not here to discuss me, remember?"

I sit in the chair, he indicates, Kaipor standing beside me, his hands on my shoulder, since the chair has no arm for him to sit on. It's one of those fold-away chairs with a metal back and a padded brown seat.

Mr. Simon accepts my obedience. I suppose, being a police officer, he's used to it. He nods almost imperceptibly, then picks up the phone, pushes in three different numbers, and orders, "Bring in a couple of bottles of water and a witness for the statements I'm going to take." Then he hangs up without a "please" or a "thank you."

"Was that your secretary?" I ask. "Don't you ever greet her with a "hello" or . . ."

"I don't have time for that, Clea. This is a police station, not a debutante's ball."

I sigh. Kaipor pats my shoulder. I dart a look at the freestanding lamp next to me. It makes me feel like I'm in a military prison. I wonder if the bright lights will glare into my eyes when the questioning starts.

The man who steps into the room carrying bottled waters and a steno pad is very handsome. He has hair the color of new-laid tar and clear, olive-tan skin. His nose is regal . . . princely.

Then, when he opens his mouth and grins at me with a perfect smile and speaks with the most adorable British accent, I melt completely. This new cop has movie star charisma.

"Clea, this is Officer Basheer Hussain. He's on loan, so to speak, as he learns the ropes around here."

I hold out my hand, and he takes it with the same gentleness I see mirrored in the softness of his coffee-brown eyes. The skin on his hand is soft, almost womanish, but there's nothing soft or womanish about the rest of him. Basheer Hussain is a good six feet in height, broad-shouldered, and as masculine as any adulating female could desire.

You will disconnect at once, my travmeb, Kaipor orders sharply.

My *travmeb* is silly to speak so sharply. I would have dropped the handshake in another minute or so, I think. Yet, although our tactile connection is severed, Basheer's eyes still peer into my soul, and I can't look away.

Kaipor does not appreciate my admiration. Without my noticing, he apparently rams his foot down on Basheer's toes. The poor man is suddenly hopping up and down, holding his right foot and crying out in a steady stream of foreign-sounding mumble-jumble.

You will disconnect at once, my travmeb, Kaipor orders sharply.

He is silly to speak so sharply. I would have dropped the handshake in another minute or so, I think. Yet, although our tactile connection is severed, Basheer's eyes still peer into my soul, and I can't look away.

Kaipor does not appreciate my admiration. Without my noticing, he apparently rams his foot down on Basheer's toes. The poor man is suddenly hopping up and down, holding his right foot and crying out in a steady stream of foreign-sounding mumble-jumble.

Return to your seat, Kaipor demands.

I raise my chin and glare at him. I won't be told what to do. Kaipor should know that.

He does, but it doesn't keep him from dragging me over to the chair and pushing me down into it. Once seated, he holds me there, both hands on my shoulder.

It is not proper for you to romance an Earthy, he says, deliberately mispronouncing the name and sounding angrier than I've ever heard him.

"Romancing?" I yell out. Then I notice that Basheer has stopped dancing, and although his mouth is still open, it's no longer babbling foreign-sounding words. Detective Simons is watching me, too. His mouth is closed, but his eyes tell the same story as Basheer's mouth. They both think I've flipped my lid.

Darn you! I explode at Kaipor. *Go away!*

At the same moment, I mind send the thought, I remember vividly how I asked Kaipor to come with me. I start to humble myself by saying I'm sorry, but his response shocks me into silence.

I will not leave you to open yourself to this stranger. Your behavior has upset me greatly, Strata. You and I will discuss this later, but for now, I shall simply enforce my role as your travmeb, doing whatever I must.

I close my eyes to avoid having Basheer or Detective Simons read my face. I shut my mouth, too, making sure I don't reply out loud to Kaipor's words with something verbally acidic. I can see that I've already baffled both men. I can't imagine what it must have looked like when Kaipor half-dragged me back to my chair. Then my sudden outburst — no wonder they're looking at me like I've sprouted three noses.

Detective Simons comes out of his amazement first. He raps a pencil against his desk, calling us back to attention. Then he says, "You want to hand that water to Clea, Basheer?"

The man doesn't act like he wants to come anywhere near me, but he steps closer, cautious as a watchful tiger.

I did not really hurt him, you know, Strata, Kaipor states.

I have nothing to say to him. I'm too angry. "Thank you, Basheer," I tell the man as he stretches out his hand and offers the bottle to me.

When I take it, and nothing happens to him, Basheer's smile lights up again. "You are most welcome, lovely Clea," he says, evidently forgetting that a moment before, he was viewing me as some kind of monster.

Tell him you are spoken for. Tell him that you have a lover and that amorous advances are not suitable.

Stop it!

I'm irked with Kaipor, but not as angry as I was a moment ago. After all, Basheer may be movie-star exotic, but he's not the one who saved me from Clarence's intentions at the graveyard. He's not the one who risked his life to turn into a Leoreon to avoid frightening me by masquerading as a Prezvaght.

It was because I love you, Kaipor reminds me, following my thoughts as I mellow.

Just then, Detective Simons clears his throat and says, "Shall we get started?"

As if his words are magic, Basheer collects a folding chair that is hiding behind the far end of the desk. With the grace of a dancer, he unfolds it and slides down onto it. I can picture him sitting on a flying carpet cross-legged, cross-armed, and naked chested.

I can picture him atop an elephant, riding through the jungle. I can even imagine him striding through that same mist of greenery, one hand atop a Bengal tiger, the other arm holding a falcon or a hemp-woven basket in which a spitting cobra lies buried inside its coil.

"Clea," Detective Simons says to get my attention again.

My eyes are reluctant, but I pull them away from my absorption in the handsome Basheer. I admit that Kaipor's hand squeezing my shoulder may have something to do with my twisting my head around to look at Detective Simons.

"First, I want you to tell me the story in your own words, Clea," the detective says as he pulls out a tape recorder and starts the machine.

My eyes rest briefly on the red button of record, yet I hear as if in the distance, the detective's voice completing his directions: "Tell us what happened that day, Clea, from the start of that séance to the final moment when you were knocked unconscious on the steps of the mausoleum."

For a moment, I panic. How can I explain everything without mentioning Kaipor? My eyes flit to Basheer sitting there on that wobbly folding chair, one just like mine, yet he sits it like a prince, perfectly at ease, with the memo pad in front of him, his left hand holding an ink pen, waiting to write down every word I say.

Feeling my regard, Basheer looks up. "Do not be afraid, little miss. We only wish to record your words. I promise it will not hurt, Clea," he says, giving me a smile that could instantly turn brown sugar into syrup.

Kaipor's hands on my shoulders tighten. I'm very aware of his watchfulness. I look away and begin to speak.

Chapter Eight

"I stood in that crowded room, knowing that something awful was going to happen. I don't know how I knew that, but I did. Sometimes, it's like you can just feel the shadows of bad. They reach out with their long, skinny fingers, grabbing at you, waiting to pull you into it."

"Yes, I have felt that too," Basheer says when I stop speaking.

Detective Simons gives him a look as if telling him to be still, but I smile at the officer. It's good that we share that feeling. I go on, knowing that at least Basheer understands.

"What happened then?" Detective Simons nudges.

I try to swallow, but my mouth feels parched. I twist the cap of the water bottle until it cracks open. Then I lift the bottle and drink. I restore its top, urgently needing a moment to calm my nerves.

Tell them about the Ouija board, Strata.

I nod, forgetting for a moment that the others cannot hear Kaipor's whispers. I look up. Their eyes haven't grown suspicious again. They think I nodded only at the memories.

Detective Simons checks the tape recorder, but I can see, even from across the room, that it's still running. Besides, I can hear its hum, just like I can hear Basheer's pen scratching softly when he makes his odd, little marks across the paper.

"We had assembled for a séance, as you remember, Detective Simons. We were going to use the Ouija board. It was supposed to name Tom's murderer. Julia, the ghost, had told me she would guide my hand, but she didn't have the chance because Clarence feared the Ouija board too much. He believed in it. That's why he stopped the séance before his name was completely spelled out."

I pause to close my eyes. I've reached the part that frightens me. It's not nearly as awful as when I was at the cemetery, but it's still bad because this is the part where Clarence touched me.

"I hardly remember how it happened. I thought Clarence was across the room, next to you, in fact, but then, without warning, he was suddenly grasping me, clamping me tightly against his body. He was whispering things, too, horrible things. He told me he was glad he killed Tom. He said Tom deserved to die."

I stop then, waiting to hear if Detective Simons will add something, but he doesn't. He motions me to continue. I glance at the tape recorder and then at Basheer. They are both ready to hear my words.

I sigh a very shaky breath. Kaipor squeezes my shoulder gently with his right hand. His hands have loosened, yet I feel the warmth of them on my body. They reassure now, not restrain.

"What else did Clarence say?" Detective Simons asks.

"Nothing. Not then. Not to me, anyway. At least, I don't remember, except . . ." I break down then, too emotional to go on. I've just remembered far too vividly all the horrid things Clarence said to me later, how he was going to entertain himself at my expense, what he was going to do to me . . .

Detective Simons stops the machine and stands up, then strides over with a hankie. It's a big white man's hankie. I take it and use it thoroughly, blowing and wailing like a ninny.

"This is too much for her, can you not see," says the gorgeous Basheer.

I want to tell him that it's okay, but I can't stop crying. Even Kaipor's arms around me don't halt my tears. It's almost like my words have brought Clarence into the room. I can hear his filthy whispers. I can feel his hands pawing me.

No, you're safe, my love. Feel my arms around you. Nothing's going to hurt you again. I don't care if the Council tears off my wings; I won't allow you to be harmed.

That, for some reason, strikes me as funny. I giggle in the midst of my tears. Wings? You don't have any wings, I sob.

It means my ability to flit about wherever I wish, my darling. It has absolutely nothing to do with my physical appendages, he explains, giving me a quick kiss on the cheek.

I am aware that the others are watching. Kaipor has kneeled on the floor in front of me. His arms are pulling me forward slightly. My head is down where he can kiss it. Can the men hear the sound of Kaipor's kisses?

Please, Kaipor, I say, pulling away from him, scooting myself properly back into the chair.

"Would you like a cola or a cup of coffee?" Detective Simons asks when he sees my tears subsiding into the spastic, hiccough-filled remnants of fading emotional distress.

I nod. "A cola?" I ask.

Basheer, without a word, rises and exits from the room. I hope he's going for a soda. I've finished the water, and my mouth is dry again. I feel like I've walked for hours in the desert. I stand up and stretch, and then it hits me. Before I get the cola, I need to use the john.

That problem is quickly solved. There's one down the hall. I open the single door and proceed in. I return just as Basheer does. He grins and holds out an icy soda.

"It is good to remember that when something evil has transpired, it must be let free from its crevice inside the soul. It needs cleansing to allow you to begin again. You must purge this Clarence, expelling his evil. Then you will be free to start your life again."

I agree with him, Strata. Tell the police what they want to know. Pour it out until every drop of harm done to your goodness is removed. Then you will heal.

They are both saying the same things. It's so easy for them. They haven't endured the pain of it, the terror, the conviction that death had arrived. I could recognize the theoretical value of their words, slap it down, lay it to rest, end it, and move on. That's Dr. John's viewpoint, too.

When an attempted rape is over, for them, it's simply over. Yet it isn't. It never is. Because it's in every nightmare, in every restless move a man makes who's sitting too nearby. The truth is that rape awakens a knowledge that innocence never realized, that no one is ever truly safe.

I've only taken a few sips of my soda when Detective Simons turns the tape recorder back on and urges me to complete the story of how I ended up at the cemetery with Clarence.

I can't remember exactly where I left off, so I start with the mad rush of the guard dog attacking me because it thinks I'm trying to escape.

"The Doberman turned out to be one of Clarence's pets, so it doesn't hurt me," I explain, "but I've never been so scared in my life. I thought the dog was going to tear me to pieces."

Not even when the Prezvaght came? Kaipor asks.

All right. I was more scared then, but I can't mention them.

"That dog wanted to attack, but Clarence ordered it to sit, and it did. But its eyes never stopped watching me. It wanted to kill me."

"Wasn't that the same dog you befriended last week? I heard you and Demon took off for the woods. Where were you heading, Clea? How did you and that dog become friends?" Detective Simons asks.

"I guess Demon just remembered me. He was friendly that day," I answer, not knowing what else to say. I can't tell Detective Simons that I talked with the dog. He'd never understand.

"Why did you try to run away, Clea?"

I shake my head. "I didn't, Detective Simons. Where would I go? The Institute is my home."

He looks doubtful about that, but then he points to the tape recorder and waves me on with my story.

I sigh and continue. "Clarence decided to bring Demon along. He said the dog could guard me. So he put Demon into the backseat where it growled every time I moved.

"How did your hands get tied? Did Clarence do that at the cemetery?"

"No, he pulled out his shoestrings right there in the car. Then he tossed his shoes in the back, just missing Demon. He tied my wrists together with one shoelace and used the other on my feet."

I keep talking, attempting to describe everything, closing my eyes, sometimes, to recall exactly the progression of events. Detective Simons stops me to demand explanations, to question each detail.

Finally, I'm done. I sit back on the chair and breathe in deeply. I feel like a sponge someone has wrung out with extremely rough twisting. Maybe they've even poured bleach over me, for Basheer claims that I've been thoroughly cleansed by my lengthy tale.

It's late. Detective Simons says that I must wait while he speaks with the captain. I don't question that. I just sit, exhaustedly drying out, so to speak.

Detective Simons leaves the door open as he walks off. I can see policemen walking by, their black leather boots pounding the beat of whatever their official business is. Not one of them moseys or meanders. They walk like they work, like busy army ants, conducting individual tasks they've been programmed to do.

Basheer, oblivious to my thoughts, at first stays in his chair. But after a moment, he stands and moves over to Detective Simons' desk so he can better examine the notes, perhaps checking them for errors. Then, when the detective still hasn't returned, Basheer looks up. "You are a very brave woman," he tells me.

I don't want to call him a liar, but there really isn't much bravery inside me. Besides, when someone holds a gun to you, you really have no choice about a situation. You can't collapse and say, "I give up. I'm too scared to move. Kill me."

That wouldn't have impressed Clarence anyway. He would have just picked me up and carried me. In fact, he did at one point. That was when he was commenting that I was as light as a small child.

That's one thing that Zoey and I argue about. She thinks it would be wonderful to be petite, which is her name for my puniness. She claims that men adore small women. I tell her that if that's true, it's only because they can push us around easier. Julia agrees with me, but Kaipor doesn't. He says size doesn't matter, that he'd love me even if I had Zoey's mass.

I guess he would. Would Joe have attacked me if I'd been six feet tall? Would Clarence have?

Size makes no difference to a Dirzaght. If the Council approved it, I could change my shape to please you, Strata. Would you like me to be smaller than you are?

I shake my head. Kaipor would always be the same no matter how large or small his body appeared. Maybe size is only in the mind. I suppose it's partly how you see yourself.

"You are all right?" Basheer asks as he stands up and walks toward me.

I nod. It makes me nervous to see him coming closer. I don't know what Kaipor will do. I'd back away from Basheer's advance, but I'm still sitting, and my *travmeb's* hands are resting on my shoulders.

Basheer comes even closer, then he squats down beside me. He makes no attempt to touch me, however. With his eyes looking up at me, he says, "I have given good advice, Clea. You must not dwell on this past. Do you understand?"

He's already said that, Strata. Do you want me to give him a good kick?

I shake my head, responding to Kaipor, but Basheer thinks I'm answering him. "No, you must accept what I say is true. You are too young to dwell on evil. I ask you to believe me in this. I am older than you. I have seen such things. Your people should not have left you alone."

"But I wasn't alone. Detective Simons was right next to me . . ."

"A young woman must be sheltered from such men. Her family must gather around her protectively."

"My parents are dead," I tell him sadly.

"Your aunts and uncles, then. Where are they?"

"I only have one. My uncle is the one who committed me," I tell Basheer, shrugging as if the fact doesn't hurt anymore.

"He turned his back on one so lovely? I would never do that. I would . . ."

"Are you proposing to Clea?" Detective Simons asks as he stands in the open doorway, laughing. "I leave you for a minute, and look what happens. Have you stolen my assistant away from me, Clea?"

Basheer jumps up with such haste that it's as if he were caught raiding the cookie jar. "I was only providing the young woman with good-hearted advice. She is alone with no one to care for her. It is a difficult situation. Who will speak for her?"

Does he think you have lost the capability of speech?

I don't answer. I am too tired. I know Detective Simons is teasing. So is Kaipor. But I don't want to hear more advice or jokes. I just want to go home.

It is not your home, my darling travmeb. Your home, when we are finally permitted to return there, is Dirzaght.

I sigh. Dirzaght doesn't really feel like home. It's alien, foreign, too strange to even consider as home. Yet, timidly, I touch my stomach and think about the child Kaipor and I will have one day. When Threll is born, I will have to face abandoning Earth. I don't want to. The truth is that I don't really want to leave what has come to be my home world.

A few minutes later, when Detective Simons decides to take me back to the Institute, we walk through the long maze of closed doors where off-duty officers meander about as if all city crime has come to a halt. A couple of men nod to the detective. All of them scrutinize me with searching eyes as if implanting my face on their inner billboard of "the most wanted."

We pass the chief, the one with the cola-stained front. He waves with one hand, but the glint in his eyes as he stares at me wears suspicion, as if, for some reason, he's attached me to his "accident." I drop my eyes so he won't read guilt in them. Is throwing soda on a cop the same as "assaulting an officer"? Motive, means, and . . . is it method? The means was an impossibility. Does that count?

Outside, Detective Simons opens the door of a new black and white. I guess we're not returning in the old plug of a car he was driving before. I sit down in the police car, trying not to breathe in the smell of formaldehyde from its newness.

I glance toward the rear. The rifle is missing from its holder. My eyes search to identify other pieces of equipment that I've heard of. My eyes take in the scanner. There's a velocity box, too. I recognize that from a pamphlet I'd picked up at the counter when we passed by. It's a new system the department is testing to tag car speeders.

Detective Simons settles down into his seat. He looks over to check that I've buckled up, but of course I have. I pull at the strap to prove it. He nods and starts the engine.

I watch as he places his arm on the back seat and starts backing. I study him in his new setting and decide that he matches this car better than the other, even though he still has his plain clothes on.

I sigh. Detective Simons glances at me, smiles, and then flips on the siren. I wince a half-smile but cover my ears with my hands.

"Okay. No siren," he says, laughing. "But you're not going to get all moody on the way back, are you?"

I shake my head. I didn't even know I was being "moody." Is silence a sign of grumpiness? I sigh again, even heavier than the first time.

"Look at me, Clea," he orders.

His order startles me, not with its direction, but with the intensity of the tone. My eyes meet his.

"Clea," he says, sounding like he's about to tell me something horrible. "Tell me you haven't fallen in love with Basheer. You haven't, have you?"

I burst out with the giggles. I can't help myself. I know that Kaipor's back at the station still exploring, but I figure that he'll probably pop in at any second, so I don't dare tease Detective Simons. Kaipor doesn't always understand such things. So, I attempt to suppress the giggles and shake my head.

He exhales. "That a girl. It wouldn't be the first time, I'm afraid. Something about the way the guy looks . . . or maybe it's his accent. I don't know, but girls get all moony eyed over him."

"Not this one," I say quickly, just in case Kaipor's anywhere around. "He is nice, though. He acted really concerned."

"Yeah, he's a good guy, all right. A bit extreme about some things. He's a liberal who thinks the working class should be giving up half of our salary to support the poor and needy. He and I don't speak the same political language. That's for sure."

I nod. I'm not really sure what Detective Simons is talking about, but at least he's not drilling me about Clarence. That's a relief after the hours spent in his office.

We're driving down Main Street. I look out the window and notice a woman passing by with a small French poodle. The dog has pink bows on its ears and polka-dot booties.

"Look at that," I exclaim.

The detective glances over. "That's Mrs. Caruthers. She walks her dog every day and changes his attire just as often.

"And they think I should be locked up?" I kid, but the joke goes sour when Detective Simons gives me one of those strange looks of his, inhales sharply and starts in on lecture number 247.

For the rest of the way back to the Institute, I hear about how I have to stop talking about aliens and prepare myself to live in the world.

I stare out the window, watching the scenery pass by. A black and white cow lifts her head and watches us drive by. *Good flavor to the grass today,* she says as we drive by. I gape.

"Problem at the Shaara Dairy?" Detective Simons asks.

I close my mouth and shake my head. "Just an old cow chewing her cud. I was wondering why she was out by herself," I lie.

Detective Simons gives me another look, but at least that stops the lecture. We ride in silence until we arrive at the Institute. The gate admits us, sliding open with a well-greased and silent mechanism. It's as if someone's watching for us because Detective Simons doesn't even have to give his name before we're allowed in. I suppose being in a police car blocks a lot of questions.

When the car stops at the front door, I figure I'll just jump out, but my side is locked. The handle doesn't open the door. Detective Simons, I'm sure, could release the lock, but he doesn't. He opens his door, slides out of the seat, and comes around. Then he clicks it, and my door opens.

"You don't have to walk me in," I tell him, but he's already moving up the stairs. Maybe it's his responsibility to turn me over to Institute personnel. Together, we climb the steps and enter through the massive front door, and Dr. Schmidt strides forward, swinging out his hand to greet the detective. "Get what you need?" my psychiatrist asks.

I must be invisible, I think to myself, but I say nothing, aware that it's just the politics of the place. On the totem pole, we mentals rank on the bottom. I suppose that makes sense.

Staff and visitors are on the same level. They're sane. They don't hear dogs and cows talking to them.

How boring, says Kaipor, slipping into my mind again.

Chapter Nine

We patients thought Dr. John was officially gone, having departed to work at another hospital, but he pops back in one day at breakfast, Dr. Paulson at his side.

"All right, ladies and gentlemen," Dr. Paulson begins speaking, but we're all so excited to see Dr. John that Dr. Paulson has a very tough time getting our attention. Finally, Dr. Paulson picks up a metal serving tray, clearing all the bananas and apples from it, and clangs at it with a spoon. Bong! Bong! We have no choice then. All eyes swing in his direction.

"Thank you, ladies and gentlemen," Dr. Paulson says as if he were an announcer at a ballgame instead of a psychiatrist.

"What ladies?" Joe snorts, drawing forth a ring of guffaws from the males around him.

Melanie, Zoey and I give Joe a look that's supposed to indicate that he's equal to the grime under dirty fingernails. He sneers back, but his eyes appraise me, and he whistles in a sexist way.

I ignore him, but Kaipor, who vehemently dislikes Joe, manages to stage an "accident" in retaliation. One of our servers, the very sweet but mentally slow Cora, drops the plastic pitcher of orange juice she's just picked up to take back to the kitchen. Naturally, it falls right on Joe (although he's at least two feet away from where she was holding it.)

Kaipor, I yell. *Stop it!*

All right, he says. *I'm finished anyway for today. That jerk still hasn't figured out that you're hands off.*

Hands off? Where do you pick up these expressions, Kaipor?

From you.

Joe is wiping away the mess, the other guys are half-sliding off their chairs laughing at the scene, and Cora has run off in tears. It's a big flare-up, but Dr. Paulson simply bangs once more at the metal tray.

"Ladies and gentlemen," he says again, clearing his throat with the grave sound he makes that usually means he's about to sing.

"I'm here this morning to tell you some great news. Dr John and I have written a grant, which is for you."

None of us know what a grant is, but we clap politely. The guys around Joe whistle through their fingers and cheer louder than anyone, not because they care about whatever Dr. Paulsen is talking about but because they like to make noise and will do so with any excuse.

Dr. John stands. "Quiet down. Quiet down," he says, flapping his hands like a bird treading air in slow motion.

Dr. Paulson turns and nods, thanking him, then continues. "This grant gives us the opportunity to put on a melodrama starring YOU."

Zoey and I look at each other, then at Melanie. "What?" is the whispered word on all our lips.

A play with a hero, a heroine, and a nasty villain. People will boo and hiss the villain. Sounds perfect for Joe.

"Did you hear that?" Zoey says, her eyes wider than donuts, her mouth a small basketball hoop. "Was that Kaipor?"

Melanie has the exact same expression on her face. I laugh. "He told you what a melodrama is? They both nod, looking, frankly, rather scared about it.

"We have decided to allow each of you to audition for the parts," Dr. John says, his eyes scanning the patients at the table. "We'll need someone dedicated enough to learn all the lines for Sergeant Ricko, the handsome hero, and for the villainous Mr. Blout, and, of course, for our lovely female lead, Miss Sugar Pie."

The catcalls start up again. Joe scrambles out of his seat and says, "Doctors. Pray tell. Will the hero get to kiss the lovely Miss Sugar Pie? And how about the villain, does he get to?"

Dr. John studies Joe for a moment. "You would fit the character of the villain better, Joe, I believe. However, to answer your question, both characters actually kiss the lovely lady. His eyes flit to me, and he tilts his head as if already indicating that I have won the part.

"Remember, everyone is going to participate. Do you hear me?" Dr. Paulson says. "Each of you will have a part in the production. There will be no laggards."

"Well, that leaves me out," says one of the older men at the foot of the table. His comment really doesn't make much sense. We all turn back to the psychiatrists, eyeing them with incredulity, all thinking the same thing — everyone?

"Any questions?" Dr. Paulson asks us, his eyes scanning us as if already marking his cast.

We don't have any questions. We're too stunned.

I don't want you playing Miss Sugar Pie if you have to be kissed by both a villain and a hero, especially if one of them is Joe, Kaipor tells me.

My chin goes up, and my brain reverses itself. A moment ago, I was ready to say, "No way," to the melodrama, but with Kaipor's words, quivering like an unbroken egg yolk, I stand up, walk over to the pile of play pamphlets the doctors have left for us on the table, and pointedly pick up one.

"Bye," I call out. "I'm going up to my room to learn the lines for Miss Sugar Pie. This sounds like fun."

Zoey shakes her head at me. Melanie only sighs. "I wish I could do that," she says, "but I can't memorize. Besides, there's no way I'd let someone kiss me . . ."

"Are you kidding?" Zoey laughs. "That's the incentive for learning all those lines!"

As I walk up to my room, I'm prepared for Kaipor to start arguing with me about doing the play, but he's strangely quiet.

"Hey, Clea," Zoey calls out from behind me. "What will you do if you have to kiss Joe, throw up?"

I stop and look back at her. Joe is standing not two feet away. His eyes are watching me. He's grinning. "You can count on me kissing you, Clea. I intend to make the most of it, too."

I waver then, suddenly unsure, but Kaipor blurts out, *Ask him if he enjoys orange juice baths. Remind him if he bothers you in any way, something bad will always happen.*

I'm not going to say that, I humph.

"You like orange juice baths?" Zoey says suddenly. "Every time you bother Clea, something bad happens, doesn't it?"

I whirl around to look at her face. Her eyes are bulging. Her hand is covering her mouth. She looks at me and shakes her head. "I don't know why I said that," she says.

I nod. I do.

"What are you talking about, Blubber Lips?" Joe retorts. Then his eyes flit about as if he expects something terrible to happen to him. When nothing does, he relaxes. The usual smile curves one side of his mouth. "See. It was just a coincidence before. Nothing's gonna happen to me, nothing but having a real, good time with Miss Sugar Pie.

Then he winks and turns. He almost makes it to the exit, but the carpet runner has been flipped over. I see it a moment too late. Poor Joe. He trips, lands on his belly with a splat, and turns to glare at Zoey.

"Thanks, Kaipor," Zoey whispers into the air.

~~~

The next day, I memorize the lines for Miss Sugar Pie all the way through the first act. The thought of delivering the words and showing all the girl's moods on my face doesn't bother me in the least. In fact, I'm looking forward to that part of it. I think it'll be great fun to pretend to be someone else. But as I read through the whole play, I discover that Miss Sugar Pie has to sing. That part makes the butterflies in my stomach do cartwheels. Sing?

Jackie, the heavyweight aide, knocks at my door and tells me that she's come to take me to the tryouts. I think if the psychiatrists had sent anyone else, I would have backed out. I know Jackie won't take "no" for an answer. She'd probably just throw me over her back like a bag of laundry and carry me down the stairs.

I know the song I'm supposed to sing, and I suppose it's in my range, but I've never sung in front of anyone.

"Why, you have a sweet voice," Dr. Paulson says after I do my best to keep up with the tape-recorded music.

"You will have to sing louder, though," Dr. John tells me.

So that's that. I know I can't project my voice. I don't have that kind of confidence. I shake my head. "Thanks anyway. I appreciate you letting me have the opportunity to try out." I turn and start to walk away.

"Hold it!" Dr. John yells. Dr. Paulson darts to my side to bring me back.

"Oh, no, you don't," Dr. Paulson says. "We chose this script for you. You're perfect for it."

"But you said I'm not loud enough."

"Then we'll hook you up to a microphone. It will amplify your voice just fine," Dr. John says, laughing at my attempt to escape.

"In fact, we're counting on you to carry this play, to be honest, Clea," Dr. John adds. "We have a lot of confidence in you. You've got abilities you haven't even started to tap. Maybe this melodrama will open up some of them."

It's always good to hear someone offer praise. It makes up for all the disparagement one heap on one's self — almost. Yet, their compliments also, in a way, make me feel ill at ease. How can I possibly live up to their expectations? Me, carry the whole melodrama? I've never even been in a play before. I tell them that, of course, as I nibble on my lower lip, trying to imagine what it will be like on stage with an audience of people.

You will do an excellent job, Kaipor tells me. *I have faith in you.*

Although it's nice to have Kaipor on my side, sometimes I feel like his opinion doesn't count. Should I allow an invisible person to determine my level of confidence?

"We chose Stan to play the hero who saves you," Dr. John says, reading his notes as if he can't really recall who won the part.

"Stan?" I close my eyes, trying to recall which male they're talking about.

"He's rather old for the part, I'm afraid," Dr. Paulson remarks, looking thoughtful. "But he will be superb. His voice is quite wonderful."

"Old?" I feel like the parrot repeating their words, but the truth is, I'd figured that the hero would be Joe. The idea that it's not, that it's someone I don't even know, surprises me.

"When do I meet him? And when do we start practices?" I ask, finally getting my tongue to speak in more than a single syllable.

"Stan?" I close my eyes, trying to recall which male they're talking about.

"He's rather old for the part, I'm afraid," Dr. Paulson remarks, looking thoughtful. "But he will be superb. His voice is quite wonderful."

"Old?" I feel like the parrot repeating their words, but the truth is, I'd figured that the hero would be Joe. The idea that it's not, that it's someone I don't even know, surprises me.

"When do I meet him? And when do we start practices?" I ask, finally getting my tongue to speak in more than a single syllable.

I don't have long to wait. Stan and I have our first practice the next day. He greets me with "I see God smiles through your eyes, young lady."

I have no idea how to respond to that, but he gives me a goofy smile, showing laugh lines around his eyes. I adore laugh lines. They show that a person has spent a whole lifetime of being good-humored.

While I'm thinking about that, Stan takes my hand and says, "I'm delighted to get to work with you on this project," and he kisses the back of my hand.

I shoot a look at Dr. John. I'm suddenly not comfortable, but when he notices my expression, he only laughs. "Stan is harmless, Clea. You will find that he's far more interested in converting you to God's goodness than in sedu . . ."

Dr John stops suddenly when he sees Stan raising a hand to stop his flow of words. "It is not wise to bathe the ears of the virtuous in the water of sin," Stan tells him sternly.

I smile then. I like the man. The feeling must be mutual because he once more takes my hand, then leads me over to a nearby chair and asks me to sit beside him for a moment.

"Please allow us to have time to become better acquainted," Stan orders the psychiatrists. Both men are busy talking about some details in regard to the play. I don't think they'd care if we vanished temporarily, but Dr. John nods. Dr. Paulson doesn't even look up. His hand merely flaps, indicating for us to go ahead.

"Tell me about your relationship with the Lord," Stan asks me, breaking the ice right off.

I think a moment, wondering what I should say. "My parents never attended church, and I don't really know that much about stuff like that," I tell him.

"Stuff?" Stan's face breaks out in a layer of fine perspiration. He shakes his head and says, "We must pray together. That's the first step."

Melanie always gets down on the floor to pray. Zoey invokes God while standing up. I'm very interested that Stan doesn't move at all. He simply closes his eyes, raises our hands in the air, cupping them open like we can hold more spirit that way, and then he begins to recite the Lord's Prayer. Melanie taught that to me several months ago so I speak the words with him, enjoying their flavor, loving the part about the Lord being my shepherd and walking with him next to still waters.

When the prayer is over, Stan talks on and on about the Lord's great wisdom. Kaipor pops in and tries to chat, but I shake my head. I want to hear this. Stan speaks such beautiful words.

Kaipor's eyes grow brighter. He peers into me. Then he smiles and nods. *These are the same words they speak on many, many worlds, my travmeb. I have heard such wonders before. You are correct, my love. The melody of them is the song of truth no matter where they're spoken.*

So saying, he kisses my forehead, then sits down at my feet, one hand on my knee, his eyes watching and listening.

When Stan finally runs down, both Kaipor and I agree that Stan is inspirational. We have both enjoyed listening to him.

We start our melodrama practice for real the following day. Stan is sweet and very patient. And as Dr. John and Dr. Paulson said, my hero's voice is a dream. When Stan starts singing the first time, I dissolve into a puddle at his feet.

He laughs and picks me up, not pausing a moment in his love song. When he sings to me like that, his eyes reflecting his affection, his voice so deep and baritone, I think I'm almost in love.

Of course, I don't let on that a mere love song can influence me like that because Kaipor is always breathing over my shoulder, attentive at all times. He likes Stan, but I don't think he trusts anyone around me.

Ever since I got pregnant, Kaipor had become even more protective than he used to be. I guess I do understand that somewhat. If Kaipor were crooning to some other girl or she was singing love songs to him, I might be just as green-eyed with jealousy.

Anyway, because of that, I'm very careful to keep my distance from Stan, even though I don't think Stan would ever let me do anything more. When he gives me the peck of a kiss at the end, even then, he puts nothing into it. He treats me more like a little sister more than someone with whom he'd ever want to become romantically involved. His eyes light up only when he's talking about the goodness of the Lord.

He and I practice all the scenes where we're together, but the villain has never once shown up. I don't understand why. I keep asking if the doctors haven't chosen someone to play the part. They tell me that they have and then give me another excuse about why he hasn't come to play practice. I don't know why they're keeping the villain's identity such a mystery. Why can't I know who it is? Why all the secrecy? (I'm sure it's Joe, after all.)

The play is scheduled for a week from Friday. Most of the patients have been selling tickets. Dr. Schmidt bought one from me and so did Detective Simons. Dr. John wanted to know if I wasn't going to call my uncle, but I didn't bother to answer him. I don't know whether Dr. John meant the question as a joke or whether he just doesn't understand the relationship between my uncle and me. When Dr. John asked me that, I started wondering what ever happened to the investigation Detective Simons was launching into my uncle's background. Did it get dropped? I plan to ask him if he comes to the play. I hope Mr. Simons attends.

I've practiced my part with a lot of the patients. Melanie is my best friend in the play. She's the one who encourages me to fall in love with the handsome Sergeant Ricko.

Unfortunately, Melanie is a lousy actress. She forgets her lines over and over, and she mumbles the ones she knows. I keep prompting her as we do our lines together, but she hasn't gotten any better. I doubt she's going to improve before the show.

I can't understand the difficulty. A play unfolds like a jigsaw puzzle. It's always the same. You simply match the pieces to each character, and the shape of it forms the whole of the puzzle. Then, each time you recreate it, the acting part gets easier and easier. But Melanie doesn't see it like that. She doesn't live the character. She only thinks about the people watching her, and that she has to remember her lines. Poor Melanie.

Zoey is fantastic as the character of my mother. She always carries a handkerchief and twists it round and round. Zoey was originally told to play the part seriously, but she somehow always makes it funny. Sometimes, when she starts making her faces and overly exaggerated body movements, I think I'm going to "blow" my lines because she makes me laugh so hard. I know Zoey's going to be the star of the show. She's wonderful!

As I said, I've practiced every scene, but Dr. John has been the villain in all the practices. It's so hard to treat him as the bad guy. I imagine Mr. Blout as being ugly and ungainly. Dr. John is the opposite of that. The watchers only giggle when he does his evil laugh. It's like Mickey Mouse suddenly snarling. The two images just don't work.

When will I ever get a chance to see the real villain? Why hasn't he come out of hiding? Why all the mystery? Even for the dress rehearsal, the real actor doesn't show up. What's going on?

Then, the day of the play arrives. I don my pink gingham dress and stand ready to go on, never once having met the real Mr. Blout. We're all standing around talking about that. We feel cheated and not ready to give our best! But it's too late to back out. The audience is assembling.

What if our villain is too cowardly to show up? What if he forgets his lines, having never practiced them with us? What if he makes me look like a fool?

I am pacing, but Kaipor stops me. *Calm down, my love. You must relax.*

He forces me to drink a few sips of water. (He's always making me drink water.) I comply, but then I push the bottle away.

I don't want water. I want a villain!

The curtains open, and I enter. My "mother" and I go through our scenes. Just like I thought, Zoey has the audience chuckling away. Good. At least the people like the play. Now, what about the villain?

Then the evil music starts playing. The audience boos as the villain comes on stage. It's obvious he's out there, center stage, but I'm still behind the partition of the house so I can't see. Who is it? Who's the villain?

I hear his boots clamping on the ground. He walks heavily as if he's a two-hundred-pound he-man. The knock comes. I open the cardboard door. I should have known. How could I have doubted? It's Joe, of course.

"I have come to trade your mother's debts for your hand in marriage, my dear," Joe says with a sinister snarl. The audience boos again. Joe is just right. He turns and gives them the evil eye. Then he laughs. Shivers run up and down my spine. He's good all right, and the character fits him to a "T."

"You cannot spurn me ever again, Miss Sugar Pie, for I hold your mother's life in my hands," he says, showing me her bills. "Will you send her to debtor's prison, or will you marry me?"

Zoey falls down, sobbing.

"Oh, mother," I say, wrapping my arms around her. "What shall I do? Oh, what shall I do? Tell me, please."

The music sounds, the dark, somber melody of the villain. I know that Mr. Blout is supposed to be playing with his mustache. I hear him turn to the audience and tell them how he will force me into his arms by brute force if I refuse him.

"Boooooo," the audience roars, then hisses most appropriately.

Joe strides over to me and jerks me up. "Kiss me," he cries. "You're mine."

But just as the moment those slobbery lips are about to touch mine, my hero comes dashing in. Stan saves the day — at least that one, for there are many more such moments in the play.

The curtain falls, and the audience stands up, taking their intermission break.

"Why didn't you practice with us?" I hiss at Joe.

He laughs evilly, still in character. "I love a little mystery," he says, grabbing me right in front of the others and kissing me soundly on the lips. No one moves to defend me. I think they're all too shocked. I struggle, kicking at Joe's shin, but he's too strong for me to break away and too agile for me to make contact with a foot.

Just then, as if we were still in front of an audience, and right in the storyline, Stan saves the day. Since he's bigger than Joe, Stan peels the villain off me like a banana peel, then lifts me up in his arms and carries me off stage. The whole crew cheers.

"Thank you, Stan," I say a minute later as my hero sets me down.

He smiles. "God loves you, sweetheart," he says as he walks away.

The rest of the play, the one that takes place in front of the audience, goes perfectly. I don't have to pretend I don't like the villain. It's in every move I make.

Later, everyone tells me how perfect my gestures and my facial expressions were. But that wasn't acting. I meant every hateful thing I said.

The only mystery to it all is how the play ends without any of Kaipor's retributions. That comes half an hour later.

The play goes so well, that afterwards, the audience gathers around us, and both Mr. Schmidt and Detective Simons give me bouquets of roses. I sniff the fragrance and smile. I'm ecstatic that the play met with the audience's approval, and that I survived my kiss with Joe, during which nothing awful happened, especially at the hands of Kaipor.

Then I see a face I'm not expecting. My uncle has come to the melodrama. As if he feels my glance, he looks up, then heads toward me, his eyes staring into mine. I see no smile on his face, no friendly greeting. I tremble, afraid.

"Well done, niece," he says stiffly. "However, I was surprised not to see aliens in the production. Have you given them up at last?"

Dr. Schmidt and Detective Simons are standing there, but my uncle ignores them both as he glowers down at me. I sigh, wishing he hadn't come.

"How nice to see you again," Detective Simons speaks up, not offering my uncle a hand to shake. "Didn't Clea do a great job?"

"Clea, you were absolutely wonderful," Dr. John interrupts, coming up behind us. "Oh, I see your uncle is here. Perfect. Weren't you impressed with Clea?" Have you ever seen a big, black cloud hovering over the sky, and then the sun peeks in and moves it aside? That's what happens when Dr. John comes over. The dark ugliness in my uncle's face clears, and suddenly, he brings out his fake smile. Because of Dr. John's presence, I notice my uncle doesn't bother to answer Detective Simons. He just turns his charm on Dr. John.

"Yes, you've done wonders with her. She was always a pretty little girl. It's such a shame she's so violent."

"Violent?" the two doctors repeat.

"What would you call a girl who kills her own parents?"

I take a step back, one second away from running, but Dr. Schmidt stops me with a hand on my shoulder. "You must face him, Clea. Stand up to him now. Tell him the truth."

"I have told him," I say limply, tears already starting their travel down my face.

"Clea," Stan says, coming up behind me. "You were magnificent. Why are you crying?"

"She doesn't like being reminded about being a murderer," my uncle says, making the horror of the moment even worse.

Stan's eyes circle the group. "Clea? This young woman is a fine Christian woman. What are you talking about?"

I will do whatever you want to this idiot uncle of yours, Strata. Just name it, Kaipor says.

"I never murdered my parents. You know that. You were there, weren't you? You saw it happen," I say, suddenly recalling something I hadn't remembered before.

The room stills. All conversations have come to an abrupt stop as everyone centers their attention on our small group.

"What do you mean, Clea? You never said your uncle was there. Was he at the house the day your parents were murdered?" Detective Simons demands.

You haven't answered me, Strata. The council won't allow me to kill him, but anything short of that.

No. No violence, I answer Kaipor. Then I stare at my uncle, starting to remember it more clearly.

"You were there. I saw you, but you showed me a watch on a chain. You told me that would help me. You moved it back and forth. I remember now."

"He hypnotized you?" Detective Simons mutters under his breath.

"Yes. I see it. I remember now. I understand what he did. He told me he wasn't there, but he was. He saw the Prezvaght."

"I never saw anything," he cries out angrily. "The girl's crazy."

Stan moves closer. "Have you confessed your sins to the Lord, brother?" he asks my uncle.

"Get this loony bird away from me!" my uncle cries out, but Stan doesn't move. He simply stares as if he can see inside my uncle's soul.

"Satan owns you. You're the devil's spawn," Stan declares, and he takes two steps back, lifts up a cross, and holds it in front of him as if he's warding off a vampire. "You must burn in Hell. Give me the matches Dr. John. This is the true villain, and he must burn."

"Easy, Stan," Dr. Paulson says, leading the man away. "It will be okay. You were great in the play. Tell me about . . ."

Wow. I think I know why Stan is in the asylum with the rest of us. He's a firebug. I let out a breath and forget about the dashing hero of the melodrama and focus again on the man Stan called the spawn of Satan.

I swallow and look harder. My mind is digging deeper, probing the oozing sores of my past. Could it be? Could my uncle have convinced me that I saw aliens? Could aliens be something he hypnotized me into believing?

Strata, my darling, you know that's not true, Kaipor says, hugging me around the waist. *Remember our walk in the woods? Remember what I taught you about speaking to animals? Remember our many nights together?*

"What else did you hypnotize me into believing?" I demand of my uncle.

"I didn't hypnotize you. I don't even know how to do such a thing. Doctor, you need to put Clea into tighter security. She has too much freedom here. All these people are being exposed. What if she turns suddenly and attacks them like she did with her parents?"

Kaipor lets go of me. I whirl around to see why I've been released so abruptly. But I know. In the sickness of my stomach, I know Kaipor didn't listen to me. He's had enough of my uncle and has decided to take revenge.

"No, Kaipor," I yell out, but it's too late. He's disappeared. I feel his absence. I know he's no longer in the room, but where has he gone? What is he doing? Is he going to do something bad?

"Calm down, Clea. We aren't going to let your uncle continue these accusations. I think Langston's investigations into your uncle's finances, actually, your finances, Clea, have shown quite a few discrepancies. "

"What do you mean? What are you talking about? It's my right to handle the girl's money. You can see for yourself that she's a loony. What discrepancies?"

Detective Simons takes over then. He lifts up his briefcase and takes out some papers. "I am serving you with a court injunction, Mr. Sautern. You will no longer have access to your niece's money, and I'm giving you a warning. There is a full inspection going on right now concerning all the monies you have spent from her trust."

It's a nice moment. Just seeing the look on my uncle's face is enough for me, but then someone calls out, "Hey, there's a car on fire."

With a sick feeling in my stomach, I meet my uncle's eyes. Instantly, we both know whose car they're talking about.

All of the guests go running outside to make sure it's not their car that's being destroyed. Most of the patients scurry over to windows to gape and discuss the scene in the parking lot. I hear the sirens of the arriving firetrucks. I assume the firemen in their shiny yellow Kevlar coats will deal with the situation quickly.

Since there's gasoline in a vehicle, I imagine the firemen will be spraying the car with the white foam used for a class B fire. For a moment, I want to join the spectators standing at the window. It would be interesting to observe all the action for research purposes. Such visual details can add distinct veracity to a story, but I am super tired. I need to rest my brain, free from the amped excitement going on around me.

I turn to face the stairs. Climbing the steps takes the last dregs of my energy.

We were supposed to get a huge fancy cake as our reward for having acted in the melodrama, but I presume that's either been delayed or canceled. I am glad that the elaborate cake cutting celebration they would have insisted I take part in is not going on right now. Feeling sick inside from my dealings with my uncle, small talk and cake would absolutely finish me off. In fact, the very idea of cake makes me want to vomit.

It is incredibly comforting to return to my room. Kaipor, probably having decided that I'm furious with him for setting my uncle's car on fire, is hiding somewhere. The psychiatrists will have to deal with an insurance broker and the police — and my uncle, who is no doubt blaming me for the destruction of his car.

Detective Simons, after giving me the strangest look, as if he suspected that I'd had a hand in it in somehow, had probably returned to the station. Of course, I'd been standing in front of him at the time, so he'd have great difficulty trying to prove that I had anything to do with it.

I hope everyone stays busy for the next few hours. I feel like an empty battery would feel if it were conscious: completely and utterly depleted.

I hang my costume in the closet, wash off my stage makeup and plop myself down in my computer chair. Then I set my fingers on the keyboard in preparation for a stress-relieving story.

Ah, what did people do before the Internet? I wonder as I kick off my shoes and wiggle my toes. How can people live without the warm fuzzy comfort of its stimulation? I sigh with contentment, roll my neck to get rid of all the day's tension, and click on the writing site.

Nine messages? Wow! Someone likes my latest story about the unicorn and the alien! I chuckle at their comments, respond to the reviewer, and then read some of their stories. One of them is sad. Tears are stroking my face when Kaipor pops in.

Don't cry, my love, he orders.

I jump a foot off my chair. *You scared me!* I tell him as I wipe my eyes and reach for a tissue. *Oh, I just read the saddest tale. I can't believe the man deserted her like that. She had a child, too. How could he do that?*

Who are you talking about? Kaipor asks, pulling up a chair. I start to explain, but he yanks me away from the computer as if what I'm doing has no importance.

Are you angry with me, my darling? He demands, his eyes a flame of heat, his arms so tight they're almost bruising my skin.

Stop it, I tell him, and break away. *Of course, I'm angry. You had no right to set his car on fire. My uncle's a jerk, but that doesn't mean you . . ."*

I love you. That gives me the reason, Kaipor says, full of rage. *I won't stand by and see him abuse you like that. You have dealt with too much of that. You deserve better.*

"I can take care of myself, Kaipor. I don't need you to descend on my enemies like that. I want . . ."

I know what you want. You want to stay here, curled up in this superficial world. You're too good for this, Clea. You're not crazy. You need to break free.

"I see aliens. Isn't that crazy enough?" My anger is already sputtering out. I drop down on the edge of the bed and place my hands over my face. I can't bear to see the look in Kaipor's eyes. I don't want to see the hurt because I've rejected him again.

"Kaipor, I don't know if I'm crazy or not, but lighting people's cars doesn't help me to figure it out. My uncle's going to think I did it somehow. Detective Simons thinks so, too. If people believe that I'm dangerous, I'll never be free from this place. Don't you understand that?"

Kaipor sits next to me. At once his arm is curving about me, like he can solve all my problems just by holding me.

I am sorry, my travmeb, he says, kissing my forehead and my cheeks. *Maybe I should not have done that, but worms proliferate on this planet. No one stops them. I only wanted to protect you.*

I sigh. Sometimes, I think Kaipor is as irrational as I am. Why else would he solve problems with violence? Why else would he think that impregnating me would improve my life?

Or had he even cared how I'd feel about it? Was being in the good graces of the Council more important to him than whatever I was feeling? These are questions I've been asking myself more and more.

You are still angry, he says. *Let me soothe it away. I shall kiss the unpleasantness goodbye. I shall take your body into the spheres where such things are unimportant.*

As he's speaking, his hands are punctuating his words with promises, but I don't want that. Not now. I bolt up, pulling away from him.

"Leave me alone, Kaipor. Go away. I want to try living without you. I want to see if I can . . ."

You're sending me away? His hands have latched onto me. He spins me around to look at him. The muscles in his cheeks have tightened. His right eye is glaring at me.

You are still a child. You do not understand the nature of the travmeb or how lucky you are that I was the chosen one. I am patient with you. Do you think all travmebs would be equally so?

"I don't know. I don't know anything about them, and you won't tell me," I scream at him.

Lower your voice. You will bring the guards and your friends. You will cause the hospital to be plunged into chaos again.

"No. They'll just think I'm talking to my alien friends. They won't pay any attention, will they?" I spit out with such bitterness, that it surprises me.

What do you want from me, Strata? Kaipor asks, returning my anger with coldness. *What more can I do to show my love?*

"You can leave me for a while. You can let me grow up without hovering around like a specter, like a guard, like a chaperoning parent."

Kaipor stares into my eyes disbelievingly. But I'm so angry, I'm meeting his gaze full force, even though, deep inside me, I know that I can't see beneath their surface. And right now, the brittle hardness of them is like ice.

There is great violence in Kaipor. I can feel it. He has powers I've never even seen. He's stronger than I am, smarter, older . . . Yet my anger simmers as I watch his eyes probing mine. Have I gone too far? Is the ice cracking? Am I about to plunge underneath?

Despite my anger, I begin to tremble. Suddenly, I'm afraid.

All right, Strata. So be it, Kaipor says with a voice as chilly as a winter's morning. He drops his hold on me, blinks once, and fades away.

I return to the Internet, but I sit there staring at the screen. In a moment, the tears come. They wash all my joy away.

Chapter Ten

The weeks snail crawl by. I write stories almost every day. I do my daily homework tasks, finishing up every subject to perfection. The teacher has no choice but to fork over good grades, all A's, of course. Only the SAT remains, but I know I'll do well. I've studied hard. I'm ready.

Two colleges have already given me a pre-acceptance, depending on how well I do on the big test. My teacher, begrudgingly, helps me with the practices. But she's unhappy because now that I've finished everything, she's unemployed. I think she was secretly hoping I'd flunk.

A tester is coming out to the Institute to administer the SAT to me. That's in three weeks. I gather the testing site is not happy about having to do that, but Dr. Schmidt tells them they must meet the needs of people with disabilities. I'm sorry about that. I think I really could have gone to the high school where it's being offered to the public, but maybe it's better this way. I'm not as confident as I used to be, not now that I'm alone. You see, Kaipor has not come back.

I'm in my fourth month of pregnancy. I'm fatter now, but my clothes still fit. The nurse says that I'm right on schedule — not having gained too much. I still have no other signs that I'm pregnant, however. I eat and drink whatever I want, and I sleep just about like always. (I don't tell the nurse that I lie awake every night wishing for Kaipor's arms. How could I tell her that?)

The nurse says that they're going to take me to the hospital next week for an ultrasound. I don't understand why, but when I ask her, she avoids my eyes. "I don't think anything's wrong," she tells me. "We just want to make sure the baby is doing well."

That worries me. I go back to my room and look up "ultrasound" on the Internet. It's also called a sonogram, I discover, and is not something painful at all, but pretty much just a picture of the baby. I read the other things the site tells me. It all sounds fine. I want to know everything: my baby's size, his placement, and gender, just in case Kaipor's wrong.

I am not wrong, my travmeb. But I will not allow you to have an ultrasound.

"Kaipor!" I yell and spring up to run to him, but he isn't there, or at least he's not showing himself.

Then his words hit me. "Why shouldn't I have the test?"

There will be no ultrasound. You do not need it, and it would be unwise.

"Why? Give me a reason," I yell, searching for even the shadow of Kaipor's most transparent mist body, but he's well-hidden and does not answer me. His silence feeds my anger.

"I'm going to have it done then. I want to be positive everything is all right, and since you're not around anymore, why should you care?"

But Kaipor is no longer present in my room, or at least not talking to me. I sit down at the computer and pull up another medical/scientific site. But the computer suddenly goes dead. My room lights are still on, so I know I have power. I start up the computer again, but once more, when I open the medical site, my computer goes dead.

"Are you doing this?" I call out, but Kaipor doesn't answer.

For the rest of the day, my Internet is out. I check downstairs, but theirs is fine. I write a note to Dr. Schmidt that something is wrong with my connection, but later that night, the Internet suddenly works again. However, all medical and scientific data is now blocked. I know for certain then what has happened. "Darn you, Kaipor. Stop it!" I yell, but the air is silent.

I can still visit my writing site and leave my stories for review. I can study and practice my writing for the SAT. But I stumble through the days that follow, wondering why Kaipor popped in and then left me so coldly.

The day arrives for my sonogram. I walk downstairs to meet the nurse who will accompany me to the hospital. We head toward the entrance, chatting about the baby and about the SATs I've been studying for. An aide unlocks the front door and pulls at it. Then he takes both hands and jerks.

"It's stuck," he tells us. He gives the wood a kick and struggles with the key. "Hey, what's going on?" he yells out. "Now the stupid thing won't even unlock."

The nurse's headquarters are just a few steps away. They buzz the custodian, and he comes running. He has another key, but that one doesn't work either.

"Someone's changed the lock," the man says, grunting as he works the key back and forth. He struggles for a while, but he can't get the door open.

"Don't worry, ladies," he tells us. "There are always solutions to these problems. I'll just take the old door off its hinges. That'll solve the difficulty, temporarily, of course."

So, he takes one of his power tools and withdraws the bolts from the door hinge. When all the parts are out of the frame, the man gives the door another hard tug, but it still won't open.

"No way," he says. "This is impossible. It must be Julia."

That's what everyone is murmuring under their breath, but I know the truth. Kaipor's preventing me from leaving the Institute. He told me he wouldn't permit me to have the ultrasound. Now he's making sure I can't go to the hospital to have it done.

Stop it, I demand, but the door remains closed.

Oh, of course, there's an emergency backdoor. We all go there, but the same thing happens. It refuses to open, too.

Dr. Schmidt comes onto the scene and walks up to the door. He gives it a hard kick. Then he asks for a hammer and knocks on the doorframe. None of that helps. Neither door will budge.

Dr. Schmidt scratches his head and gives me a look. I stare back at him, meeting his eyes, not volunteering what I know to be true.

"How about an axe?" the custodian suggests, but Dr. Schmidt shakes his head. "Don't you dare? We have patients that need this lock, remember? I'll call a locksmith."

"Cancel Clea's appointment. Make her a new one next week. This may take some time."

So, I return to my room and sit down on my bed. "Why, Kaipor. Why?" I ask, but again, he doesn't answer.

Later, through the gossip at lunch, I hear all about how the locksmith came to the Institute to make a new key. But when he tested the old one, he found that it worked just fine. Everyone thinks that the ghost is playing tricks. I suppose Julia could have, but I don't believe it. It is just too coincidental.

My new appointment for the ultrasound is in two weeks. When that day arrives and we try to go out the door, I guess I'll know for sure. Julia wouldn't play the same trick twice. If it's Kaipor, I think he'll do it as many times as it takes.

Why doesn't he want me to have an ultrasound? Is there something wrong with the baby, or is he afraid that they'll see it's part alien?

"Please, talk to me?' I cry out several times each day, but Kaipor doesn't speak. I want to ask him to come back to me, but I won't. It's been too long. If he really loved me, he would have returned before now. I don't want him to come back just to tell me goodbye. I couldn't bear that.

The SAT goes well. I won't know for several months how I did, of course, but I am certain I scored well. The required essays were smooth and factual. I met the word count and still had time to check my spelling and grammar. Both subjects were familiar, and I felt ready for them. I'm positive that my arguments supported my points.

Likewise, in all the subject matter, I rarely needed to pause to reflect but flowed through the test, reading and answering with confidence.

Now, I just have to wait and hope that I did as well as I think. So much rides on the results. That one test is worth more than all my years of classes, homework, and term papers.

Meanwhile, I'm still wondering why it matters. If my suspicions are correct, I won't even be here when it comes time to go away to college. Will Kaipor be the one who jerks me away? Will he fly me off on a horse again or use some other conveyance to drag me back to Dirzaght, a planet that's more science fiction to me than reality?

What if I don't want to go? Will it matter? Will the Counselors be on my side or his? They want the child, and I'll never leave our son. I know that. If the Council gives me no choice, then it's Dirzaght forever. I wish I knew for sure if I must stay there. It's not reasonable that I don't know. It's absolutely unfair that Kaipor is gone, leaving me with all these doubts and questions about my future.

Angry at Kaipor for his desertion, I ask Dr. Schmidt if I can visit the library again. The psychiatrist gives me one of his observant looks but says nothing, offering his quick nod of permission. That means, of course, that I'm planning on doing some research on ultrasounds and the possible amniocentesis that the nurse has mentioned. I don't know if Kaipor will let it happen, but I need to be ready in case it does.

Friday morning, I rise early, head down the stairs and capture Sergio. When I show him my permission card, he takes me to the library. Dr. Schmidt hasn't ordered that I be supervised. The note gives me permission to be there alone. Sergio, after a quick glance around to make sure that no one else is there, closes the door and locks me inside.

I take a moment to scan the stacks. The books' leather bindings are mostly dark brown or burgundy. It gives the library an elegance that pleases me. I breathe in deeply, enjoying the smell of refined learning. Then I walk over to the computer and turn it on.

Do you think it will matter which computer you attempt to use?

I whirl around, almost knocking over my chair, but I can't see Kaipor. He's playing the same game.

Kaipor, please, don't do this to me, I beg him.

You will not be exposed to any of their primitive diagnostics. I have told you that I will not permit it. Our child . . .

Our child? I snap. *Funny how it's our child, suddenly. You haven't been around! You're a stranger to him.*

I will not be a stranger when he's born, my dear. I figure your temper tantrum will not last much longer.

Have you ever seen someone pour kerosene on a flame? I flare up with such anger I'd slap Kaipor if I could see him.

Is that right? he chuckles and materializes. *Show me.*

But I can't because his arms have suddenly seized me in a firm embrace, and his lips are making talk impossible.

I mean to fight him, but at the feel of those arms around me, his lips touching mine, I go limp. It's been too long. I fall into his hold like an exhausted person sliding into bed.

When he releases me, I still cling. *Why did you leave me?* I cry out. *Why?*

He chuckles again. The sound sends shivers up my spine. I want him.

I think you needed me to leave, Strata, so I did as you asked. And I will disappear again if you request it. But I will never let you do what is bad for our son or for you. On that, I will not yield.

I sigh, still hanging onto his arms, refusing to let him step away from me. "Please, don't leave me," I whisper softly. "I don't want you to ever go away again, no matter what I say. Please?"

He nods, smiles down at me, and then again, our lips meet. He unlocks the library door, although it's locked from the outside. I say nothing. I'm not surprised.

Silently, we walk upstairs. No one sees us, but, of course, it wouldn't make any difference. Kaipor has faded out again, although the feel of him is substantial enough for me. His right arm is wrapped around my waist.

It's only after we've romantically and passionately reacquainted ourselves with each other that Kaipor starts to talk to me, really talk.

The child you carry was conceived on Dirzaght, Strata. Of course, his body is that of a Dirzaght's. How could it be otherwise?

I stroke Kaipor's face. I forget, sometimes, that his silver hair and features are alien. They are not alien to me. They are only the reflection of the man I love. I sigh heavily, liking what I see. Then I bend and kiss him again.

"It takes so little effort for you to explain things to me, Kaipor. Why do you so often give me demands and not tell me what I need to know?"

He takes my hand from his brow and turns it over. His lips touch my palm. His tongue paints desire across my lifelines. "You must trust me, Strata. I will do nothing to cause you harm."

"You left me alone for months!" I blurt out, springing into tears.

"No," he says, kissing away my frown. "I was here with you every moment. You were never alone. I just didn't bother you, as you'd requested."

"But if you were here, you read my longing for you. You knew how much I missed you. You could have . . ."

"The moment you told me to come back, I would have shown myself, but you never called to me."

"But I did. You never answered."

"You never asked me to come back, my *travmeb*. I waited long to hear those words, but you wouldn't say them. In the end, I took the chance. I came to you without your calling me. You still must say the words."

"Please, come back, Kaipor. Please, stay with me forever."

Once more, he kisses my hand. Then his body swings us back into action, and he rocks me again into space. This time when we eclipse, the stars nova, and the planets shoot out from hidden orbits.

I shall be taking you back to Dirzaght soon, my lovely one. Meanwhile, the Terrans must not doctor our child. Do you understand that now?

I am floating in a sea of stars, still humming blissful sighs, but I nod. "Soon? How soon? What will happen to my life here? Will I never come back?"

Kaipor, my dear Kaipor, the one who always has all the answers, doesn't respond to my question, and I read in his eyes that it's not because he's holding back but because, this time, he doesn't know the answer.

Days pass. Kaipor and I form a new relationship, one far more agreeable to me. He opens up, attempting to answer my numerous questions. Unfortunately, for as many answers as he gives me, there are countless he doesn't know.

On Wednesday, the nurse comes. I allow the thermometer at my ear and her use of the blood pressure machine that cuts off my circulation. I have no disagreement with the scale or her many questions as she records the data. Then come the fireworks.

"It's time for us to head over to the hospital for that test," she says, then adds, laughing nervously, "I've been promised that the door will open for us this time."

The nurse's name is Mrs. Torman. She wears her straw-colored blonde hair in a limp ponytail and has small oval glasses that constantly slide down her straight, ski-jump nose. I hate to disappoint her. I like the way she smiles, the gap in her two top teeth, and the sparkle in her eyes, but Kaipor is hovering beside me, floating like a ghost. He's made it so I can see him perfectly, but no one else can. He shakes his finger at me and says, tell her 'no.'

I sigh. The nurse is helping me to stand as if I can't on my own. "Mrs. Torman," I begin.

"Why, Clea, I'm going to be with you throughout this pregnancy.

I think you should call me by my first name. It's Ingrid."

I thank her and then start again. "Ingrid, I can't do this. I can't go to the hospital with you."

"You're not feeling well today, dear? Why didn't you tell me? What's wrong?" She peers into my eyes, then grabs up my wrist to check my pulse again. I don't pull away. I sigh.

What should I tell her, Kaipor?

We talked about this. Just say you don't want any tests.

Easy for him. He doesn't have to look into Ingrid's friendly and concerned eyes.

"It's just that I've made a decision," I tell her. "I don't want the tests."

"They aren't going to hurt the baby, and it will relieve your mind to know that everything's all right. We want to be sure of that, dear. It's for the best. Besides, I have the room set up for you. The technician is waiting for us. You must keep your appointment."

You don't have to do anything, Kaipor says, glaring at her, although, of course, she can't see him.

I can't bear to let people down. My eyes water and I look away. "I can't have the tests," I whisper.

Now you've done it. Why did you tell her that? Kaipor barks at me.

It's true, isn't it? I snap back, flaring at his sharpness with me.

For some reason, my words don't make him angry. Instead, he softens. His arm drapes my shoulder, and he sits down on the chair beside me.

My little love, I don't wish to be harsh with you. I'm sorry. I know this is difficult. I've asked the Council if I can take you home today or tomorrow. They've refused me again. They want you to stay longer. I don't understand why, but for now, I'm trying to obey. It's for our future, you know. If it were just me, I'd scorn their refusals and . . .

"We must take this up with your doctor, Clea. You need further tests." Ingrid's eyes have suddenly turned forbidding as the warm and friendly nurse of a moment ago recedes into those of a tyrant.

I back away from her. "I'm going back to my room," I announce, but she grabs my wrist.

"No, we're going to speak with Dr. Schmidt. He'll tell you what you need to do and explain why. Whatever has upset you, we need to straighten it out right away."

So saying, Ingrid marches me out of the room and down the hall toward Dr. Schmidt's office. I'm sure he'll be talking with one of the patients, but I didn't mention that to Ingrid. I'm listening to my *travmeb.*

Just relax, darling. They can't force you to do this. They'll probably just counsel you some more, then set up another appointment. I must get you out of here. I don't like the feel of it.

He doesn't like it? My wrist is being squeezed into a pretzel stick, and Ingrid, who I'd liked a few minutes before, has suddenly reminded me of a mad scientist bent on having her own way, even if that means blowing up the world.

We arrive at the door. Kevin is sitting outside of it, waiting to escort whichever patient is inside back to his or her room. I smile at him, but he glowers at me, thinking that I've done something horrible to upset such a pretty nurse.

This is a perfect example of how primitive these humans are. This test she wants you to have done would amount to nothing if there were any complications. The medical sciences of this planet are somewhere around first grade. The doctors have no more ability to manipulate an endangered fetus than they would perform a geosophy. They're barbaric in their knowledge, infantile, yet they have the audacity to argue with your refusal? They should be . . .

I attempt to shut out his words. They aren't very helpful to me in the current situation, and there's nothing I can do about them anyway. And what if the Council does change its mind? What if they give Kaipor permission to remove me from Earth? Can I deal with that? Can I adapt to Dirzaght?

The thought sends chills. I shut out the pain in my wrist, the look on the nurse's face, the aide's glower, and my *travmeb's* chatter about humanity's lack of medical skills, and I recall my former visits to Dirzaght. Am I ready to face that again? Am I ready to give up on Planet Earth?

Dr. Schmidt reacts to the knock on his door like an angry wind whipping at tree limbs. He thrusts open the door and blows out a livid blast of words: "Who the he…?"

Then he notes who it was that knocked. He sighs and scans the nurse's face and mine. Then he shuts the door behind him, leaving the patient inside. "I'm having a session right now. Is this urgent?"

Ingrid (or maybe it's back to Mrs. Torman since we don't seem to be close friends at the moment) drops my wrist and says, "She refuses to go. Do you understand the implications of that?"

"What? Go where? Clea?" he stutters, obviously having forgotten the whole situation.

"Your patient was scheduled for tests last week, as I'm sure you recall." Ingrid's voice is like ice cube darts. Dr. Schmidt recoils slightly.

"Ah, yes," he says. "I do remember. Of course."

"Then, as you *recall*," the nurse continues with a sharp, derisive voice, emphasizing the word *recall* as if Dr. Schmidt is equally as loony as I am. "The last time I came, the front door was inexplicably sealed shut. So not only was I unable to take this patient to her appointment, but this supposedly 'supernatural phenomena' took three hours of my time before the locksmith could declare it totally without cause.

"Now, once again, I am here to take YOUR patient to her rescheduled test, and she suddenly declares, without reason, which I suppose is to be expected since, well, I won't go into that, but, needless to say, I will not put up with this. Order her to go, and let's be done with this nonsense."

Dr. Schmidt sighs heavily and sits down on the bench next to me. Then he says, "Would you two please give us a moment?"

The nurse and Kevin slide over to the opposite end of the hall.

You better help me with this, I tell Kaipor.

He laughs. *I like the nurse's version of last week. Supernatural, huh? Isn't that what they call those human horror movies where the head revolves around and around? Maybe we should see how Nurse Ingrid looks with . . .*

Don't you dare! You know that's only a Hollywood stunt. Heads can't really do that.

"Tell me what's going on, Clea. Why don't you want the test?" Dr. Schmidt asks, interrupting.

Nervously, I try to give him my attention, but Kaipor has that glint in his eye. He's up to something, and it's all my fault. I asked for his help.

"I have reconsidered, Dr. Schmidt. The baby is perfectly formed. It has no problems. I don't need a test to tell me that."

Dr. Schmidt picks up my hand. It's very rare for him to do that. He almost never touches me. I'm intrigued.

"Clea, you don't know that the baby's all right. You see, you've been taking certain drugs . . . various medications that have side effects. We wouldn't have given them to you if we'd suspected you were pregnant. But we didn't know. I'm sorry, Clea, but your baby may NOT be okay. That's what we want to find out. We can help if there's a problem. It's not too late."

Help? In that hospital? It's rampant with staph infections. They're likelier to GIVE you an infection there than to heal you of something.

"There is no problem with my child, Dr. Schmidt. You don't need to worry. The baby's fine. Kaipor neutralized the drugs. He told me so."

Dr. Schmidt let go of my hand to wipe his brow. Then he groans. "Clea, you don't understand. There IS no Kaipor. Your child is at risk. Try to see reality, Clea. Shut out the voices you're hearing. Try."

"Kaipor's real. I believe in him. Who do you think locked the door last week? He did it, Dr. Schmidt. Kaipor doesn't want me to have those tests."

"Clea!" The word bursts out of Dr. Schmidt like an expletive, a symbol of his frustration. "You need this test. I'm not going to try to reason with you anymore, young lady. You're making it too difficult. We need to make sure the baby is okay, Clea. You have to go to the hospital."

He means they need to see if you're carrying a drug-induced freak. They want to abort the baby, Strata. They want to bring about a miscarriage.

I jump up. "I'm not giving up my child. That's what you mean, isn't it? Kaipor says you're planning to give me something in the hospital that would make me have a miscarriage. Is that the truth? Is that why I'm supposed to go to the hospital instead of just having the test here?"

"Clea, you're having hallucinations. Your paranoia is returning. No one's going to hurt you, my dear. We only want what's best for you."

"Is that what's best — to rob me of my child? That's what you were planning, isn't it? Admit it, Dr. Schmidt."

"Calm down, Clea. Calm down."

Both the nurse and Kevin, hearing the anger of my words and the increase in volume, come running back into the room.

"Want me to give her something?" Kevin asks.

"No! She'll calm down in a minute. Won't you, Clea?" Dr. Schmidt says, grabbing my shoulders and holding me until I'm forced to stand still. "Good. Now, listen to me, Clea. You're going to the hospital now, and there will be no further outbursts. You'll have this test, and then we'll talk again. You may be right that everything is okay. That's all we want to know. Nothing's going to happen today that will injure the child or you. I promise you."

I want to believe him, but Kaipor's standing behind his back, shaking his head. *I'll deal with it,* he tells me. *Go along with the doctor's orders and pretend you've changed your mind, darling, but they're not going to force you to do anything we don't want them to do. I'll see to that.*

Hearing Kaipor's words, I relax. I let the nurse walk me down to the outside door. Dr. Schmidt accompanies us. It's his hand that reaches out and unlocks the door. Then he attempts to open it, but it's stuck again.

"Darn, this thing! I told the locksmith it had swollen from the rain," Dr. Schmidt yells as he tugs and jerks at it. "Take her out the emergency door."

The faces of the nurse and Kevin don't accept Dr. Schmidt's explanation. "It's the ghost. I've heard about it, but I didn't believe it," Ingrid proclaims.

Kevin nods. "Julia," he whispers, more to himself than the visiting nurse.

"There is no ghost here at the Institute," Dr. Schmidt barks at them. "There's absolutely nothing supernatural about this situation. The door is just stuck. Do you hear me?"

So are the side door, the delivery door, and the emergency exit, just like before.

Once again the locksmith is called, but I don't go to the hospital that day. Instead, I climb the steps to my room, listening to the sound of Kaipor's laughter.

"Didn't the Council tell you not to interfere?" I ask him when we enter my room.

That wipes the laughter off Kaipor's face. His eyes grow serious. His mouth turns grim. *I won't allow you to be hurt,* he tells me once again. *If the humans push me, I'll sweep you up and away right in front of them. It's the Council's fault, Strata. You need to go home now. This place is no longer safe.*

~~~~~~~

That evening at dinner, we meet the newest addition to our lower-floor facility. A young girl, no more than fourteen years old, barely even a teen, has just been admitted. Melanie, Zoey, Carmen, and I gather her into our close-knit family and welcome her.

Danielle shyly introduces herself, and then she pours out her story. Her parents are the ones who brought her here. They say she's crazy and that she needs intensive therapy. We nod our heads and explain our similar stories. Each of us has been sentenced to the Institute by "well-meaning" relatives. Danielle smiles and acts like she's right at home.

She centers her attention on Melanie for some reason. Who knows why one person is drawn to another? Zoey, Carmen, and I accept it. It will be good for Melanie to have a new interest. She hasn't snapped back from her latest phase of collecting things, and she's still too caught up in hatred. We think the teenager will be good for her.

Danielle joins us that night in Melanie's room. We talk late, sipping colas and nibbling chips. None of us are violent, so we have great freedom. The aides have checked on us several times since Danielle's arrival. They don't know her yet, and they've been told to watch her more carefully than any of the rest of us. That doesn't bother us. We ignore their peeks and scribbled note taking. We're used to living like laboratory animals, but Danielle resents it. She rants at them, yelling for them to go away.

"Never yell at them. You have to get along with them," Zoey tells her. "They're the avenue of reduced restrictions," she explains.

"Yeah, and love, if you're in the mood," Carmen throws in, kidding Zoey about her boyfriend. Of course, that leads to an explanation. Danielle is fascinated and drags out the whole story.

"Hey guys," Zoey says after Danielle probes her too intently. "Why don't you tell her about Clea's boyfriend? He's far more interesting than mine."

Then Danielle turns her curiosity on me. Normally, it wouldn't matter, but Kaipor has formed a dislike for the new girl. He says she's too beady-eyed. I'm not sure what that means. He won't elaborate except to say: *Don't trust her. Stay away,* which he orders in his former Gestapo manner.

Kaipor still hasn't yet learned that dictating to me only makes me resentful. My nose juts up, and I ignore him, joining the others in the fun of having someone new in our group.

"There's nothing to tell," I say, "except that the father of my baby happens to be an alien."

Everyone laughs — everyone except Kaipor.

I told you not to get intimate with her. There's something not right about her, he warns me, but I block him out.

Danielle doesn't know what to think about my statement. At first she giggles, then she looks around at the others. "You believe her?" she asks.

Zoey and Melanie have both seen Kaipor. Carmen has only heard about him. She answers Danielle. "We could all use an alien lover in our beds. Don't you agree?"

"Danielle's only fourteen," I rebuke her. "Do you think that kind of talk is really appropriate?"

"Don't do the "Mom thing" with me, Clea. I haven't been a virgin for a number of years. Who is, anymore?" the girl laughs, then she props her feet up on my bed, displaying clearly the fact that she's not wearing underwear. I glance at the others, but I guess they don't notice.

Carmen steers the conversation back to the aides, filling Danielle in on the gossip about who is all right and who to watch out for. But I sit there staring at the wall, embarrassed and frankly disgusted. The way Danielle pretended to be all shy and innocent earlier and has now mutated makes me leery. I begin to wonder if there could be something to what Kaipor is saying.

She has nice legs and other parts, I must say, he teases me.

That does it. I stand up. "It's time for me to go to bed," I announce.

"What, impatient to get to your alien lover?" Danielle says snidely, darting glances around to catch the others' feelings about her quip.

Carmen laughs, but Melanie gets uptight. "They're not even married yet. It's a sin."

That takes Danielle aback. I see it in her eyes. She takes a quick survey of expressions and comes back to Melanie's comment. "You're so right. It is a terrible sin, Melanie. We must pray for her."

Melanie's face lights up. "Yes, let's all get down on our knees and pray that Clea sees the light. She's engaging in bestiality if she's sleeping with an alien. That's an even worse sin."

"Wait a minute. What are you saying? That an alien's a beast? Kaipor's not an animal. He's a man. And he's my *travmeb*, so we're married by Dirzaght standards." I say, crossing my fingers and hoping it's true since I'm still a little unclear about the meaning of *travmeb*.

Nice girl, isn't she? Kaipor whispers into my ear, his words laced with mockery. *And as to your other worries, of course, my adorable travmeb, we are man and wife. We just haven't gone through the formality of an Earth ceremony. Be kind of difficult, wouldn't it? Although, if it's important to you, I would do so. I could shape change temporarily.*

However, the relationship we have now is actually even stronger than in the Terran customs, Strata. We are tied together for centuries not mere decades.

"What's wrong with a little bestiality? It was prevalent in mythology. The tales about the bulls of Crete say ..." Carmen begins.

"We don't want to hear about that!" Melanie interrupts.

"Yes, it's blasphemy to talk about gods," Danielle tells us, wearing her innocent face again.

She and Melanie, on their knees, clutching their hands in the prayer position, start off with the Lord's Prayer. Zoey and I exchange a look. Carmen joins arms with us, and the three of us quickly march out.

As we open the door, Danielle cries out, "Let us pray for their souls. They are all wicked, dear Melanie."

We close the door, and each of us returns to our room.

The next morning, we wish we hadn't left Melanie alone with Danielle, but no one ever knows what evil might occur when you turn your back on it. No one really knows the future, apparently, not even, sometimes, a Dirzaght.

Chapter Eleven

When I get up in the morning, I remember the new girl and her strange behavior. I shiver, recalling her mood swings. There was something about her that made my skin crawl.

Then I laugh at myself. She's just a kid, fourteen years old. Raped by her boyfriend and addicted to Speed. Maybe she'll improve with time. She's probably just all mixed up. Teenagers are always prone to emotional highs and lows.

She wanted to impress Melanie. That's all it was. Or maybe she got swept up into a religious fervor just because of something Melanie said. In a couple of days, she might return to the shy, sweet girl she was when we first met her. Or so I hope.

And will the Prezvaght grow halos? Kaipor laughs.

It isn't a kind remark. He knows how I feel about those monstrous aliens, but I'm still glowing from our bed-play this past hour. I smile at him, feeling like I'm flying somewhere above Pluto. My body still tingles. "You were good," I say.

"Only good?"

"Okay, wonderful!"

He laughs again and pats my bottom. *It was fun, wasn't it?* he asks. *You're like riding one of those wild bulls in the Western Bar downtown.*

"What?" I cry out, not sure I like the comparison.

Ah, you've never been there, have you? I shall take you one of these nights. You must try it.

But I've seen movies. I know what he's talking about. The animated bull jiggles up and down and mostly throws off its riders.

"Right!" I giggle, looking down at my expanding belly.

Good point. I'll take you later after our son is born, he chuckles. *But how about an encore? This bull is ready again.*

My stomach's growling, and although my body is buzzing with the aftereffects of our mutually shared last bull ride, I've had enough. I run my hand over his face and kiss his lips, but then I dart away and run off to take a shower.

While I'm washing my hair, Zoey knocks. Kaipor invites her in. Lucky thing I don't change my mind about Kaipor's offer. Supposing I entered the room stark naked? But I don't; I'm nicely wrapped in a towel. I see my friend, grab my clothes, and say, "Be back in a minute."

I wouldn't have let her in if you'd changed your mind, Kaipor tells me, popping into the bathroom. *Want me to send her away?*

I toss the towel at him, but, of course, he's read the thought before the towel leaves my hands. I think he returns to talk with Zoey, something he's been doing more and more since he first showed himself.

When I step out, I hear the tail end of a sentence. ". . . and, we looked everywhere for them."

"For whom?" I ask, trying to catch up so I can follow the conversation.

"Melanie and the new brat," Zoey tells me. "They've disappeared. Carmen went down to tell the nurse's headquarters so they could get the aides to locate them, but honestly, they were nowhere in the Institute. We've already searched. We even sneaked upstairs and talked to Kevin. He said he hasn't seen them since last night."

"Well, there's no way that they could get out. The door's locked."

I glance over at Kaipor to see why he's so quiet. He has a funny look on his face like he's gone to sleep standing up.

"Kaipor?" I call out and then pull at his shirt. That brings him back. He looks down at me, corrals me with his arm, and kisses me soundly.

"Stop it. We have company, remember?"

Reluctantly, he lets go of me. Then he glances at Zoey. "She doesn't mind. Your friend understands. By the way, Melanie and Danielle, the brat, as you call her, are not in the Institute. I just checked."

"You can do that?" I gasp and stare at him in amazement.

"I was sure of it!" Zoey says, "Only there's something else I didn't tell you."

This is all starting to remind me of one of those thriller/suspense novels, except in real life, it's not fun to hear.

We both give our full attention to Zoey, neither of us prodding, except with our eyes.

"Remember the dress Melanie was wearing last night?"

I nod. Kaipor doesn't move. His face looks far-off again. I wonder what he's sensing.

"Well, maybe she got her period or something, but, God, this is awful, Clea, but the dress she was wearing, it has blood all over it now!"

"What!"

"She is still alive," Kaipor says, not explaining how he knows.

Zoey and I both stare at him. "How could you know that?" she asks.

"Tell us where she is," I cry, believing Kaipor can do anything. "Don't keep us in suspense."

"I do not know. She is too far away. She is wounded, though. Her life pulse is weak."

"We have to tell the nurses," Zoey yells. "We have to get the psychiatrists involved. We have to save her!"

I inhale and exhale slowly, trying to figure it all out. "What about Danielle? Is her life pulse weak, too?"

Kaipor's eyes drop to mine. He shakes his head. "She is not what she seems. I should have felt it yesterday. *They are back, Clea. The Prezvaght are back.*

"No! You said they couldn't. You said that the …"

I must leave you. I do not want to, my darling one, but I must. I must tell the Council and the Wise Ones. The Prezvaght have broken through, but not as they usually do. This is too close to you. They have come into the Institute. We safeguarded that. I do not understand. Why would they follow you here?

Kaipor, please don't go. Please.

They cannot hurt you, my love. I would never leave you alone if there were any chance of them doing so. They cannot harm you in any physical way. Their hands would burn. Their skin would fall into shreds. You are safe. Keep Zoey and Carmen with you. I will be back when I can. You are loved, my darling.

"No!" I scream. My scream goes on and on. I can't shut it out. Zoey shakes me, but I don't stop. Her hand slaps my face.

"What!" I cry out. Then I stare at her. "Did you hear Kaipor?"

"How could I? Isn't he gone?"

I nod, my eyes searching the room anyway, just in case. Then I sigh. "Before he left, Zoey, he talked about the Prezvaght. Did you hear what he said then?"

"Sit down, Clea. You're all pale. You look like you're going to faint. And, no, I didn't hear anything about that. I don't even know what you're talking about."

Kyle comes barreling through the door right then. "What the hell is going on in here?" he blasts with an angry snarl.

"It's all right now," Zoey tells him. "Clea just got scared. She saw a mouse. She'll be fine."

Kyle glowers and backs away, shutting the door behind him.

If only the Prezvaght were that easy to keep out.

They find Melanie within the hour. They say the dog mauled her to death, for Demon was loose, and blood was on his muzzle. But Zoey and I know that it wasn't Demon. It was Danielle.

Carmen comes to join us. We're sitting in the large den area. The guys are watching a game. They hardly pause at hearing the news. Melanie was never one of their favorites.

We fill Carmen in on what has happened. She was wrapped up in one of her books. She hadn't heard the news. She wipes a tear, and then we all break down, sobbing for Melanie's loss.

Joe breaks away from the game to come over. He sits down on a chair across from us. "Hey," he says. "You know, I'm sorry."

"For what?" Zoey spits at him.

"For Melanie and for what I did to Clea."

It's the first time Joe's ever said anything like that. I eye him distrustfully, but he seems sincere. I appreciate the apology, even if it took him forever to come out with it.

"Did Dr. Schmidt tell you to say that?" I ask, and he nods, looking sheepish, at least for a second.

"How did Melanie get out? Why did she leave here?" Zoey asks, not as if she's speaking to Joe or any of us, but as if she's trying to figure it out herself, and the question just rises from her lips.

"Why, you want to be doggy dinner, too?" Carmen blurts out.

"Carmen!" we shout at her. She reddens. "I'm sorry. I didn't mean it the way it came out. I only meant. Oh, hell. I don't know what I meant."

"She got out with the new girl," Joe tells us like we didn't know that. "You'll have to ask her how they did it if they ever find her. She's disappeared. Boy, she's some looker, too. I wouldn't mind a piece of that action," he adds. I throw one of the couch pillows at him. Joe catches it and grins at me.

"She's not half as pretty as you, little Clea, and despite what Dr. Schmidt made me say, I'm really sorry I didn't score with you. Someone sure did, though."

I stand up, prepared to launch myself at him. I'm that angry. Kyle, who's been watching, steps closer. "Get back over there, Joe. You know you're supposed to keep your distance from Clea."

Kyle gives me a warning look. He watches as Joe returns to the groups of guys around the television, but Kyle looks away too soon. He doesn't see Joe turn and throw a kiss at me.

"Oh, how I hate that guy," I say, wishing Kaipor were present so he could trip Joe or toss a full urinal over his head.

"Yeah? Well, he told the others he's going to marry you someday. Chris told me that he overheard one of the aides saying that Joe intended to plant the next baby. Gross, huh?" Zoey tells us.

I boil, wishing I had some of Kaipor's powers.

"You know why he says those things, though, don't you?" Carmen adds, looking at me slightly wistfully. "He's stuck on you. Don't you know that, Clea? The guy's in love."

"Right!" Zoey and I jeer before we break into laughter.

"Oh, my God," Zoey says. "I can't believe we just laughed. Melanie's dead. She's dead, you guys. Do you hear me? Last night we were with her. We were drinking colas and shooting the breeze. We were having fun. Now she's gone. It just doesn't make sense. I can't believe it."

"What are we going to do about Danielle?" Carmen breaks in on the silence that follows that. "You guys say she did it. How do you know? Maybe it did happen like Dr. Schmidt just said. Couldn't the dog have attacked her? We know it prowls the yard at night. It's possible."

"Yeah? Then where is Danielle?" I ask them. "Can you explain that one?"

"And the blood in Melanie's room," Zoey adds.

"Hey, maybe we should call that detective friend of yours. What's his name, Lang something?"

"Langston Simons," I say, repeating the name as if it holds no meaning.

"Listen, I need to tell you something," I begin, needing desperately to warn my friends. "Kaipor went back to Dirzaght, but before he left, he told me something. He said that Danielle is a . . ."

"Yes, what about me?" she says, strolling into the room as if nothing has happened.

"You did it," I yell at her, bolting off the couch. "You killed Melanie."

Danielle laughs, throwing her head back as if I've just told a funny joke. "You think that? God, you're so innocent, Clea. What would I kill her with — my bare hands?"

The others are all standing. They have moved in around me, in a defensive position.

"Where were you then?" Zoey demands. "You went outside, didn't you?"

"Sure, we took a walk together. It was a pretty night. Only I got tired and sneaked back inside. I couldn't get back to my room, though. The aides were strolling around the place. So I crawled into the basement and spent the rest of the night in there."

"You're lying. Kaipor said you weren't inside the Institute. That was this morning."

"Ah, your alien friend that no one's seen. Right. I'm sure he'd know whether I was inside or out. What's the matter? Couldn't you keep him occupied in your bed?"

"You're a Prezvaght. You killed my parents and now Melanie. What do you want? Why won't you leave me alone? Why are you here?"

Wouldn't you like to know, little spy? she whispers into my mind.

"Why, Clea. It should be obvious," she says out loud for the benefit of the others. "I'm here, just like you — because I was committed."

"That's a lie!" I shouted at her.

"Oh, really? Why don't you ask your precious Dr. Schmidt? "

He's next, sweet, little Dirzaght. And by the way, your friend Melanie was delicious.

I scream, but this time, it isn't from hysterics. It's the cry of revenge. I hate Danielle.

I'm halfway across the space between us, with fists raised and her face as my goal, when Kyle swings me up into the air and carries me out.

"No, let me go. She's a Prezvaght," I screech, but of course, he just thinks I'm crazy. They can't give me tranquilizers anymore, so he takes me to Dr. Schmidt's office and knocks. My psychiatrist is not engaged in a session this time. He comes to the door, listens to Kyle's story, and orders me to sit in my usual chair.

Kaipor isn't with me to guide me into prudence. I pour out my story about Danielle and her murder of Melanie. Dr. Schmidt steeples his hands and hears me out. Then he sighs.

"Poor Clea, this has been a great shock for you. Melanie was a good friend. I understand how it must hurt, but blaming the new girl doesn't ease the pain. The dog attacked Melanie. We know that. The vet is putting it down right this moment."

"No," I scream, remembering how I'd bonded with Demon that day. "It's not his fault. It's Danielle. She did it. Not the dog!"

But Dr. Schmidt won't listen to me. I reach out to feel the essence of Demon. He's not there anymore. He's been murdered, just like

Melanie. It's all such a horrible tragedy.

In that moment with Dr. Schmidt, my inner self clicks into place. I suddenly see that the asylum is not a warm and comfortable place. The doctors, who I once admired seem more confused and weak-minded than I am.

Perhaps the truth is that I am more Dirzaght than human. What if all this time I've been treated with massive lectures of doctor babble, confusing me whenever I saw reality, and all along, it was they who were unable to see the truth.

I leave Dr. Schmidt's office. I have not been placed in restriction since I am calm. I bid him goodbye. He does not know that I am bidding him the kind of farewell that will be forever. How could he imagine that? He is only stable in the realm that he knows. He is not Dirzaght.

As I walk out into the general area, my eyes are open to things I have not seen before. I can picture it different. I can see my friends growing in strength, leaving behind their narrowed lives. It would be possible if they were able to take the first step. That is what Kaipor tried to tell me. There is more outside, a whole world of new. One gulp of courage, a new focus, and everything could change.

I want to tell them that. I want to stir up their inner wisdoms, but that is beyond my ability. I'm too new at this, too fragile. It rests on their shoulders. Like me, they can only see what they are ready to see. They are like Langston Simons and Dr. Schmidt. Even if it hits them in the nose, they cannot accept unless . . .

Chapter Twelve

Another day passes. I continue to avoid Danielle. Dr. Schmidt abrades me for it. He says that I should make friends with her. I shake my head. "You're wasting your time. She's evil. Remember what I told you? She said she's going to kill you next."

The psychiatrist writes down my words, just as Langston Simons did, but I know that Dr. Schmidt is not really listening, not in a way that will change anything.

Joe and Danielle have become an item. She flaunts the fact that she's sleeping with him. I wonder why the hospital allows that. Don't they know what all the patients know? Danielle's supposedly a minor, which means that the Institute is liable. One word from her, and I bet she could close the place down. That would kill Dr. Schmidt, too. I wonder if that's her intention.

That night, Julia drops in to tell me that she saw Melanie's spirit. The girl was upset about the timing of her death. It seems that she hadn't taken communion and is too ashamed to rise up to heaven. I tell Julia to tell Melanie to go, anyway. No God could blame her for being murdered at an inconvenient time.

Julia looks surprised by my logic, but she nods her head and slips into the wall. I'm almost asleep when she comes back.

"Where is your alien lover?" she asks me. "Did he leave you for good this time?"

I don't want to discuss Kaipor with Julia, but it is always wisest to be polite to ghosts who can flit about wherever they please. I tell Julia that he's gone home to talk to the government leaders and will return at any moment. That placates her, but when she leaves, I can't go back to sleep.

I lie there for hours, wondering why Kaipor is still gone. I miss him so much. "Please, come home," I whisper in case he's listening, but there's no answering voice in my mind. I guess he's still in Dirzaght.

That night, Danielle tries to get Joe to leave the Institute, but he's too smart for that. So she throws a temper tantrum and declares that he raped her. She wakes up the whole Institute. We snicker behind our hands when we hear the falseness of her claim, but Joe has a history, and Danielle's a minor. The aides lock Joe into solitude, and Danielle is taken to her bedroom, sobbing as if she's truly been raped.

I wonder if they ever asked her why she was in Joe's room instead of her own. But, I suppose that will do Joe no good. He shouldn't have touched her as young as she is. Still, he's better off in solitude than dead.

I finally fall asleep around two in the morning. Julia wakes me again.

"I have to sleep," I moan.

"Yes, I know," she says. "I just want to gloat. That rapist is in solitude."

I sigh and sit up. "He didn't rape Danielle, Julia. She volunteered. She's been bragging about it all over the Institute for two days. Joe, this time, is innocent, but he'll go down for it anyway."

"Good," Julia pouts, irritated because I knew the news before she could tell me.

"Am I interrupting you, girls," says a familiar voice, and I throw the covers off and jump up to hug Kaipor.

"You're back!" I cry, kissing him everywhere I can reach. "I'm so happy! I missed you so much!"

He should look happier than he does. I realize it when he doesn't sweep me up and kiss me passionately.

I look around for Julia to entreat her to give us some privacy, but she's already taken off.

"What happened? What's wrong?" I ask, leading him over to the bed.

He sits down, rips off his shirt, and hugs me to him. *Darling, they have ordered you to stay longer. I'm sorry. They wouldn't relent no matter what I said.*

"I don't care as long as you're here with me. I don't want to leave with the Prezvaght staying in the Institute, anyway. Danielle says she's going to kill Dr. Schmidt. We can't let her do that. Please, please, help me."

Kaipor sighs and picks up my right hand. His lips travel across my palm with shivery, little kisses. I groan. I want him. I tell him so, but he shakes his head. "Not, yet, my *travmeb*. There is more I must tell you.

"There is no invasion by the Prezvaghts. The Nuro Cables are holding."

"Then how did Danielle get in?" I interrupt him. "She even admitted that she was a Prezvaght."

She's a spy, just like you are, my dear. They've planted her here to study the humans.

I read Kaipor's eyes and see that he's not telling me everything. "Why do they want to study us? Are they planning an invasion?"

Probably, but the Council doesn't believe it. They say we should wait and watch. *They do not want to go to war, Strata. I fear they will allow this planet to be overcome and still squabble over what is right and wrong.*

"I won't let that happen. But what are we going to do?"

Strata, listen to me. I tried. I argued for days, but they said that it wasn't our problem, that you're not of this world. You've only lived here a long time, and so you feel a kind of allegiance to these humans.

But you're not one of them. Remember that. You're Dirzaght, a neutral. We cannot interfere in whatever develops here, not without the Council's permission, and they won't give it to us.

I spring up and begin to pace back and forth. "This is my world. These are my people. How can you say that? I hardly know Dirzaght . . ."

Calm down, Strata. Things will change when I finally have permission to take you home. Then, the Council will give you back your cultural, spiritual, and ancestral memories. You will be fully Dirzaght again.

"No. I will always be a Terran. Don't you see? I belong here."

Report, Strata Cleadorian Flisoripar.

My mouth drops open, and I begin to speak. The words that tumble out of me are Dirzaght. *I am Dirzaght, special envoy to Stengna, Galupsia Mistoropha.*

Halt the report, Strata Cleadorian Flisoripar, but remember.

I sink down to the ground. Then I look up at my *travmeb.* I remember now. How could I have forgotten? And why?

Chapter Thirteen

I wake up the next morning to feelings I've never had before. I know that's a jaded expression, but only now do I understand it. Love blooms from moments. It opens up its petals, and the fragrance hits you. I don't care how many times you think you understand what it's all about. When that fragrance first tickles your nose and you inhale, it wakes you up. You sit up and say, "Oh, this is what it's like. I didn't understand. Not really. But now I see."

Then the colors hit you — the vivid crimsons and the dark velvet rubies. Your eyes are captured by lemon and apricot, and a multi-colored parade of sunlight-speckles dance across your vision. You rub the softness against your cheek and add texture to your wonder. Last night, when Kaipor returned and woke me to my memories, I remembered it with fresh and startling dimensions.

Love is a fine thing to possess, and it's even better with someone who mirrors that in his eyes. It's superior to every ice cream cone, every patch of grass, every tree, or bright and shiny jewel you could ever hope to hold in your hand. Love is ice water on a hot, sticky day.

I can't help these thoughts pouring out of me. Kaipor is laughing at my enthusiasm, but he's also kissing me and telling me he feels the same. Utter happiness is complete and circular and astonishingly delicious.

Zoey's knock on the door keeps me from deepening the kisses we're exchanging. For a moment, I consider asking her to go away, but then I sigh. You'll be here tonight and always?

The warmth of Kaipor's smile warms me clear to my toes. I sing as I stand up and walk to the door. I sing with the voice of birds and rainbows and sweet, gentle rain.

"What happened to you," Zoey greets me. "You're absolutely glowing. Are you sick or just deliriously happy?" She can see into the room. She sees that Kaipor has returned.

"I understand," she says, grabbing my hand. "I won't keep you. Want me to cover for you downstairs, or will you make it to breakfast?"

I giggle, but I nod my head. "I'm coming. Meet you there in ten minutes."

"Sure, you will. Morning, Kaipor," she says as she backs up and walks away.

I throw myself back on the bed and tickle my *travmeb*. For several minutes, we play at love, not like adults, but like children, splashing it back and forth and with an exuberance of touches and darting kisses. But I know it's time to get up. I've promised Zoey. I dab a final kiss on Kaipor's forehead, nose, chin, and lips. Then I rise and run in to grab a shower. Unfortunately, Kaipor follows.

In the end, Zoey is right; I miss breakfast. Eventually, I do dress and head downstairs. Bertha's in the cafeteria. She's the Institute's head cook. Always dressed in a white apron that swaddles her like a baby, she's the busiest person I know, ordering this and that, striding about the kitchen to peer into huge metal pots bubbling with something scrumptious.

But, despite her demanding job, Bertha always smiles when she sees me. Her plump face rounds even more, and she hugs me if I'm anywhere near her. This time, she sees my hungry eyes and tosses me an apple. I thank her and dash over to kiss her cheek. I wish everyone in the world were like Bertha.

"We're out of eggs," yells one of the helpers, and Bertha wheels around to solve another problem. I wave as I leave, but I doubt she sees. Her thoughts are on the missing eggs.

I find Zoey down in the large den area. She's sitting on the couch, her legs folded under her, reading a magazine.

"Hey," I call out.

"Hey," she says back. "I missed you at breakfast," she teases, her eyes full of laughter.

"Love is kind of nice, don't you think?"

She frowns. "I wouldn't know. Chris hasn't dropped by lately. I guess he's gotten tired of crazy."

Zoey is saner than the rest of this world, Kaipor tells me, his hands dropping down to rest on my shoulders as if they were part of me and belonged there.

"Did you hear Kaipor?" I asked. "He says you're saner than the rest of this world."

Zoey lifts up her eyes and smiles, but she can't see Kaipor, so she's not sure where to direct her smile. She ends up looking off to the side.

"He's standing behind me, Zoey."

"Who's behind you, dear little Clista?" Danielle says.

I don't answer her, but Kaipor's hands are suddenly claws clamping down on my skin. He catches the thought and removes them. Then he gently pushes me over to the couch. *Sit down, Strata. Let me deal with her.*

I put my apple down on the table in front of the couch. I've suddenly lost my appetite. I'm picturing what Danielle really looks like and what she did to Melanie.

No one's in the room but the three of us. I guess that's why Kaipor figures it's okay to materialize. He unfolds himself into reality and stands glaring at Danielle.

"You will leave my *travmeb* alone. You will abandon the Institute as your feeding ground. You will depart NOW," he orders.

Danielle merely looks amused. She places her hands on her hips and glares back. "Dackor, peacemaker of the Dirzaght, I spit on you."

Danielle, in a moment of intense anger, transforms into her real shape. Then, regaining control, almost in the same breath, she returns to the human casing. Zoey latches onto my arm. "Did you see that? Did you see what she just did?"

"It's her real shape," I whisper. "She's an alien, Zoey, a Prezvaght."

"I protect the friends of my *travmeb*. You will not do more damage here," Kaipor warns her.

Danielle begins to laugh. "I have only just started. Your mate caused us much embarrassment. She interfered. My people died when yours came to defend her. Why was she here? She had no business. Those humans were marked by us long before the treaty. They were ours."

"They were my parents," I shout, bolting up. I grab the apple and throw it with all my strength. It knocks Danielle in the forehead, but she doesn't even flinch. "Child of the Dirzaght, I would love to rake my claws across your pretty, white cheeks. Blood would improve your complexion."

Kaipor balls his hands into fists, but he doesn't move forward. He draws in a breath and opens his fists to hold his temper in abeyance. "The Council is aware of your presence here. You are being watched. The girl, Melanie, was not your property."

Danielle shifts, rocking back and forth on the balls of her feet. "It was self-defense, oh, peacekeeper. The girl attacked me out in the garden. What else could I do?" Danielle says with a wicked grin.

"The Council has filed a complaint. Her death may be yours."

"I doubt that. Meanwhile, what could be more delightful than to tease the child-spy of the Dirzaght? It pleasures me greatly. But this conversation grows tedious. I have hunger pains. I believe Dr. Schmidt might be getting some fresh air about now. Bye."

"No," I yell, running forward to stop her. Kaipor halts me. "Do something. Please!" I cry out.

My love turns to me, his eyes sallow with bitterness, and he shakes his head. *I am Dackor, Strata. She has reminded me that despite what my fists and my heart wish, I am bound. The Council has forbidden me to kill her. She is right. I cannot interfere.*

Strangely, Kaipor's inability to act does not repel me. It makes me love him more, for I understand. In fact, I wish I were still unable to do violence, but I've lost my former passivity. I am a warrior now, flooded with the memories of the brutality of the Prezvaght.

"I will stop her," I shout, and I break away from him and rush out of the room. Zoey and Kaipor follow.

I've never been sports minded. No karate in my family, no boxing, no wrestling, but as I sprint after Daniel, I assess everything I know. The front door is open. It's our hour of permitted outdoor activities. I dash through the door and out into the sunshine. But Danielle has already disappeared.

"Did you see the new girl?" I ask one of the guys. He's supposed to be pulling weeds, but he looks like he's spending more time playing in the dirt than being useful.

He looks up at me. "Clea," he smiles, showing off a mouth minus teeth.

Noticing my stare, he closes his lips. "I forgot my teeth. Whoops!" he says, grinning a simpleton's grin.

"It doesn't matter, Gregg. You're handsome without them."

Gregg is one of the older guys, a man with an I.Q. so low that a sick joke currently running the gamut of the Institute says that one night, Gregg got lost going to the bathroom and ended up sleeping on the floor. If you knew Gregg really well, you'd also figure that it's probably not a joke.

But he's a sweet man. His only vice is his infatuation with hugging people.

And that, suddenly, gives me an idea. It's a sick idea, even worse than the joke, but I have to do something. Danielle isn't a large girl, but she's bigger than I am. (Everyone's bigger than me.)

"Gregg, there's someone I want you to hug. Is that okay?"

This isn't wise, Strata. He could get hurt.

Any other suggestions?

Gregg's grin is fully covering the bottom half of his face. He puts down the trowel he was holding clutched in his left hand, stands up, and wipes off his hands on his pants.

"Okay," he says, bobbing his head up and down.

The two of us (well, three of us, if I count the invisible Kaipor) head out in search of Danielle. We're just in time. She's found Dr. Schmidt and is using her wiles on him to steer him away from the group.

"There's the one you need to hug, Gregg. See her?"

Gregg takes off running. He seizes Danielle from the back and wraps her up in arms that probably even a Prezvaght can't untangle.

Meanwhile, I run to Dr. Schmidt and drag him back toward the group. "You can't wander off. I warned you that she wants to kill you. Where was she leading you? Why did you go with her?"

The psychiatrist is barely listening to me. "Gregg," he calls out. "Let her go."

I'm afraid the guy is really overly enthusiastic with his hug. Perhaps that's my fault. He's hugging Danielle tight enough to reformat her bone structure — if she were human. She reacts automatically for her own self-defense. She transforms. It's only for a second. It allows her to break away, but Gregg sees her change, and so does Dr. Schmidt.

"I need to sit down," he whispers. "I've gotten too much sun out here."

Gregg backs away from Danielle and runs toward us. "She-monster," he yells. "She-monster."

I calm him down. Dr. Schmidt doesn't even pause to listen. He's collapsed under the huge oak tree, fanning himself and repeating over and over, "Too much sun. That's all it was. Too much sun."

"What plants were you working with?" I ask Gregg.

The question causes Gregg to forget about Danielle. He takes my hand and pulls me back over to his flowers. "Reds and yellows," he explains. "Pretty reds and yellows."

I nod while keeping an eye on Dr. Schmidt. Thankfully, Danielle has given up for today. She stomps off, back into the Institute, glaring at me with needle-pricks of anger.

I compliment Gregg's pretty flowers. He bends down and continues his weeding, smiling as he shows me each nasty weed he's pulled. I praise him and edge away.

When we're outside, the cafeteria always brings out several pitchers of lemonade. I walk over, pour a glass, and head back to the oak tree where Dr. Schmidt is sitting.

He is a non-believer. He will get over it quickly, Kaipor assures me. *You did well, my travmeb. I am proud of you.*

Thanks, but I can't protect Dr. Schmidt every time. I need help. I need the Council.

But I have told you. You are not endangered. They will not intercede for humans, not against one lone stray Prezvaght, spying, as we do.

But the difference is that we don't kill humans. Prezvaght do.

"Here, Dr. Schmidt. Drink this. It will help," I tell him.

"Why, thank you, Clea. How thoughtful. Yes, this is just what I needed. The heat does strange things to a human's mind sometimes. You didn't see anything funny, did you?"

Don't tear at his disbelief, Strata. He will mind-collapse if you do.

A psychiatrist? But I look down into his eyes, and I can see that Kaipor is right. Dr. Schmidt would not remain sane in a world of aliens. He is too rigid.

"I saw Gregg hugging Danielle. Is that what you mean, Dr. Schmidt?" I ask him.

"Is that all you saw? No aliens today?" he tries to joke.

"There are aliens all around us," I tell him. The birds, the worms in the soil, the insects buzzing under this tree. None of them are humanoid, Dr. Schmidt, so I suppose they are aliens."

He laughs then and sips his lemonade. "You are such a bright young girl, Clea. We must make sure you get accepted to a good university."

Not if I have anything to say about it. You will be heading home, not away into an even more dangerous environment.

What could be safer than sleeping under the same roof with a Prezvaght? I laugh, trying not to let the sting of Kaipor's words about my education rouse me into anger.

I'm sorry, my darling. I forget sometimes how important going away to the university is to you. A coming-of-age rite in this land, I believe.

No, the road to the future, I say, but then I wonder if that still applies to me when at any moment I could be transported off to Dirzaght.

"Hey, the game's on. Let's go. Everyone inside now!" yells Kyle, and the men all jump up and go running towards the Institute.

"Is it football or basketball today?" I ask Dr. Schmidt as he boosts himself up and starts heading for the entry.

He gives me a funny look. "Clea, you never understand about the games, do you? It doesn't matter which one it is. It's the sport of it that counts. Men are playing against men. The team spirit. The roar of the crowd. The thrill of the timer counting off the minutes."

I sigh. He's right. I don't understand, but I walk inside with everyone else, allowing the birds to reclaim their quiet yard.

It's chicken a la king for dinner that night. I nibble at the vegetables and wish that Bertha cooked every meal. The other cook believes that anything he puts meat in has all the flavor it needs. I take another helping of asparagus and grab a roll. At least there's the usual fruit bowl. I consider it, wondering whether to take a tangerine or a banana. I take both and start on the banana first.

While I'm munching, Danielle watches me steadily. I notice that she spurns the fruit but ladles heaps of the chicken a la king onto her plate. Her strange, green eyes flit about, probably choosing her next victim. I try not to think about that, but even in her human husk, she's creepy. I shiver.

"You cold?" Zoey asks.

Danielle sees my reaction to her as well. Her tongue whips out, and she wipes her mouth with it. Her tongue is twice as long as a human's. I glance about me to see if anyone's noticed, but everyone is busy eating. Danielle sneers. Then she laughs.

We continue eating until all the food is gone. Talking usually comes after the meal as we wait for the dessert to be brought in. So, other than the sound of the clicking utensils as they cut and scrape and meet teeth and open mouth, the room is quiet — at least until Danielle stands up and steals everyone's attention.

She looks in my direction, which causes the patients to glance at me, too. "Well, I want to congratulate all of us. Despite Clea's avowals, we actually survived another day without an alien takeover."

The others cheer. The guys whistle since Danielle is posing suggestively. My cheeks flush. It should mean nothing to me if they laugh, yet their jeering eyes are like a sea of arrows. I flinch. Then I drop my eyes.

"Don't look down," Zoey says, kicking my foot. "Don't let her win. She's ridiculing you; give it back to her."

"I'm not into mockery," I whisper back. "I hate barbed words."

"Yeah, well, you should hate her. Look what she's doing. They think she's hot. They don't know she's just hungry."

I look up and study the room. Zoey's right. Half the guys are panting, wanting her.

Stay out of it, Kaipor orders me as I start to stand up. *She's evil. You're sweet and innocent. Do you think you can compete in her game?*

Whose side are you on? I demand, then I push him aside and lurch to my feet.

"You'd be funnier, Danielle, if you weren't selling yourself to the loudest laugh."

"Oooh!" laughs one of the men, catching on to what is going down. "Fight! Fight! Fight!"

Kevin steps closer. "Ladies, let's sit down and decide to get along, shall we?"

I'm watching Danielle's face. She's not at all interested in pleasing the aide. She could care less about Friday movies and other Institute carrots. "Oh, you delicious man! Kevin, didn't I satisfy you well enough before dinner? Are you back for more?"

The men go wild. It's their kind of talk. Kevin backs up, a look of horror on his face. "I never touched you. I wouldn't either. You're a . . ." He stops, not completing the thought.

"Did all of you hear what she did to Joe?" Kevin asks them. "He's locked up in solitude because he played around with this girl. She was willing, too, as I heard it. He's going to jail, men. He's out of here, not because he deserves it this time, but because she's underage. Who's going with him? Which one of you wants to leave all this behind for one hop in Danielle's bed?"

"That will be enough," Dr. Germoni says with a voice like a hard-edged steel plate. He is late for dinner. He should have been there all along, but now he plays catch up, giving Kevin a scornful look for his words. Then the doctor turns the same look at the rest of us, trying to decide which ones he will send to the dungeon.

Dr. Germoni is the newest doctor at the Institute. Most of us haven't even met him. After the look we're getting, we're all wishing for our easy-going songster, Dr. John. As the psychiatrist's eyes travel, staring at each person in the room, noting them, examining them, checking them over as if he can peer inside their souls, he makes his way toward the table my friends and I are sitting at.

"Sit down, girls," he snaps at Danielle and me. I don't wait to see if she will obey him. I slide back into my chair. For the moment, the new psychiatrist scares me more than the Prezvaght.

But he doesn't scare Danielle at all. She simply licks her lips. "A new doctor?" she says. "Have you heard why psychiatrists don't like to work together?" she asks the group.

No one answers. Why bait the crocodile when it's only inches away from one's nose?

"Do you know, Dr. Germoni?" Danielle queries, turning her moss-green eyes towards him.

"I would imagine it's because they're always too busy to converse," he tells her, sitting down stiffly on a chair at the head of the table.

"Why, no," she laughs. "You see, psychiatrists shrink too fast."

No one laughs. We watch Dr. Germoni to see what he'll say. "Satire, my dear, requires a keen wit. Clowning, on the other hand, can be done in various modalities. I'm afraid your joke fell slightly flat. Do sit down, Danielle. I believe it's time for dessert."

Her eyes have turned lizard-like. Once again, her anger is causing difficulty with her body projection. Delighted, I cross my fingers that she'll lose control again, this time in front of a wider audience, but my hopes are dashed. She calmly sits in her chair.

"You are right, doctor. I should have kept to alien jokes. They are much more amusing. Do you know what you get when there are three aliens in a room?"

Dr. Germoni is reaching for the fruit bowl. He slips his fingers around a tangerine. He starts to peel it, acting as if he's not even aware of the confrontation occurring in his presence.

"Pray tell. What is the punch line?" he asks, inserting a segment of fruit into his mouth.

"How would I know? Ask Clea. She's the one who knows how the story ends. She's our alien expert."

There is nothing funny about Danielle's words. It certainly isn't a joke, but Danielle laughs so hard she gathers in the others.

I've had enough. I stand up and look about at all the laughing faces. "It ends happily, of course," I tell everyone. "All the aliens side with the humans. You see, only the Prezvaght desire Terran deaths, but then the Prezvaght are the sewage of the universe, so what else could one expect?"

Careful, Strata. Don't keep pushing her. She might erupt and do great damage before she's destroyed.

And that's worse than her picking them off one by one?

But SEWAGE? Where did that come from? Kaipor is laughing, so I think that it can't be too awful.

I'm very wrong.

"Sewage?" Danielle spits out as if tasting the very substance I've called her. "You dare to call my species — waste, garbage, ejected fecal matter? We are Prezvaght. We are the kings of the universe . . ."

She babbles on and on in that same manner for several minutes, proclaiming her kind to be the rulers, the aristocrats, the above and beyond emperor pegs of the cosmos. It grows tedious, but the changes in her hue, which start vibrating from various shadings of luminous greens to chartreuse with a preponderance for slime yellow, a hue that I think suits her best since she's as lemon sour as vomit, makes us spellbound.

Danielle's body elongates. Her arms roughen into a more scale-like texture. Her voluminous blouse pops every button and bursts forth with a chest that no human man would desire. But, I think, in truth, that few notice her chest, for everyone's staring at her face. A Prezvaght is not pretty. Its teeth are wide and broad, more like chisels than teeth, and the gray enamel on them perfectly complements that description. The sharpness of the multi-rows of beaver-like teeth brings shudders to even the strongest of hearts.

A Prezvaght nose is three-chambered and hardly there but for the triplet of openings that undulate with each breath. But I doubt that the eyes in the room are concentrating on her nose, either, for they probably can't tear themselves away from the horror of her eyes. For those, like a blasphemy against nature, are black hollowed with rings that revolve oddly.

An inner sphere peers out from its cave-like dwelling in a shade of orange so vivid, the sight of it makes some gag. The light within, flames from an inner core of fire, and casts off evil as clearly as if it were the beacon of the devil. No one who's ever seen a Prezvaght's eyes can doubt that hatred pours from its inner soul (if they have one, that is).

"You have revealed yourself to these people," I say. "Isn't that against the treaty?"

The patients' mouths are flapping like panting dogs whose jowls bounce with every turn. I ignore them. I cannot afford their distraction. If Danielle is willing to reveal herself before the patients, workers, and doctor, then everyone is in immediate danger.

"What do you know about the treaty?" she grins wickedly. "It didn't stop me from enjoying your friend, did it? Oh, I meant to ask you about that speech you're going to make, the one at her funeral. Please add that Melanie's flesh was especially sweet and tasty. I think that would give such a nice *flavor* to the occasion."

"What do you mean by that?" sputters Dr. Germoni. He has dropped the tangerine he was eating, missing his plate entirely. Fragments of an eaten piece are drooling down the side of his mouth. His eyes appear glazed as if he's about to take a step off a cliff to plummet to the ground. He's fighting that cliff, but his eyes are already taking the plunge into madness.

He turns his head to look at me. I know his question was not for me. He was addressing Danielle, but he can't bear to look at her anymore. I think again about what Kaipor told me — how delicate are the minds of psychiatrists.

We patients can travel beyond the cliff. We know how to walk on air, suspended by our slender threads of sanity. But psychiatrists don't have those threads. They live in the realm of certainty. To travel to our kingdom is an impossibility for them. They plunge. They land in quicksand. They cannot get up.

I grip the table to keep my hands from balling into fists. I want to kill Danielle for what she's done to Melanie. I have a comic book cloud hanging over my head. I know what it says. I don't have to look up to read the words. It says: *Kill her!*

You cannot, Kaipor forbids me.

But I look at Dr. Germoni, drooling like a madman. My friends, Zoey and Carmen, are glazing over, too. They're heading for that same cliff. Are their threads strong enough? Will they be like the doctor? I can't take the chance.

"Let there be war between us, Prezvaght. I plan to kill you," I tell her.

Then I pick up the pitcher of lemonade and throw it. The glass shatters against her mighty chest. The lemonade splotches her scales. She laughs, catches an ice cube, and pops it into her mouth.

Then she grabs at Dr. Germoni and with her claws, severs his head. Tangerine fragments scatter about, mingling with blood. Danielle doesn't mind. She is chewing on his left ear, her two giant paws cupping the head as an otter does his meal of fish.

Joe vomits across the table, spewing his meal. Carmen faints. Lila, one of the older patients, clutches at her heart, makes several foul noises and flops over. I stand there staring, not knowing what to do.

It is Kevin who saves the day. He has gotten a gun and uses it on Danielle. It isn't a tranquilizer gun, either. Before she realizes what has happened, green pus-like blood is already spurting from the bullet that enters her chest. Another bullet soon follows. The blood dribbles down the side of her skull. She eyes me for a moment and then grins. "Another always follows," she tells me.

Then she drops Dr. Germoni, or at least the part of him she was holding and collapses, folding inward like an accordion but with a sound far more unpleasant.

I start to race around the table to see her, but Kaipor stops me. *You must leave now,* he orders, grabbing for my arm.

I dodge around him. I must see what has happened. I must know that Danielle is dead. The others aren't moving. They are frozen in shock or perhaps insanity. I have no time to worry about them. My eyes are only for Danielle. I must be positive she's dead.

I am just in time. There was good reason to run. A Prezvaght evaporates when it dies. It shrivels as its cells turn into dust. But even those final bits curl up into finer particles, mix with the air, and fade away. In seconds, Danielle is no more. Only the half-eaten head of Dr. Germoni still lies on the ground, one eye staring, the other gone.

Kevin drops the gun and sinks to the ground. He is babbling about invasions and monsters. He'll need therapy, I know, and the Institute is now short one doctor. How will they manage? How will they get another psychiatrist to come here after this?

But that is the least of our problems. The air suddenly ripples, and a vortex lowers. Out spring two more Prezvaghts.

"What happened here?" the first one demands of me.

The second is looking me up and down. "I should have known. It's a Dirzaght and another who hovers behind her in his invisibility cloak. Come out of hiding, Dirzaght. We have traveled a long distance to find out what occurred here. You had both better be innocent of this deed."

Before I can step back, the vortex wraps me up inside, and Kaipor and I are spun off to Prezvaght, a destination to which neither of us has any desire to travel.

Chapter Fourteen

The trip doesn't last long enough to have a conversation with Kaipor. It's just a short lift-up that spins us around and around until we're too dizzy to talk, then a space of minutes while we're still recovering and swallowing hard.

But almost the moment we become aware of being whizzed through space and we're able to whisper, we exchange a quick, *I love you,* from me and a *Let me do the talking,* from Kaipor. Then, a stomach-deflating drop hits us. It's so fast a fall that we're as unsure about our final fate as if we'd stepped out to find a firing squad, frozen in puzzlement.

Plummeting from an atmospheric height (minus the heat, thankfully) leaves one with visions of becoming no more than a pool of smashed insides. Mercifully, that is not our ending because abruptly and teeth grindingly, we slow at the final moment and land perfectly and sedately on our feet.

Oddly, the first thing we hear as we lower onto the planet is not what one might expect. Prezvaght are warriors. They grind gravel in their teeth for toughness. Yet, as our feet touch the ground, a symphony of such beauty that it brings tears to my eyes greets us. A plaintive, high-pitched instrument is playing — like a violin or a flute, but neither one.

I think for a moment that it's a voice, but I hear no words, only the lovely melody, a melody that makes me think of all the sadness of the world channeled into one bittersweet, tear-jerking piece of music. As the vortex gives up its hold on me, I dissolve into tears. My body falls to the ground, and I sob.

"Good, it worked, on her, at least," a grating voice gloats so close it's almost as if he says it into my ear.

I look up. My teary face peers between two staunch legs. Kaipor has not been influenced by the music. He towers above me, defending his female-weak *travmeb*, as always. Stung as if that purposely insults me, I fling myself upward to stand beside him. He smiles at me, but it's a quick flit across his face. His gaze is on the Prezvaghts, the same ones who stole us from Earth.

"You have no right to remove us from our research. We did not injure your Prezvaght spy. I give you my word," Kaipor tells them.

"We have every right. We saw your mate standing not two of your meters from the dying Prezvaght, Danielle."

"My *travmeb* is innocent. She did not kill your agent."

"Don't waste time conversing with him," the other one intervenes. "We shall take them both to the Palace. The Craniums will decide."

The Craniums? The image of something even more objectionable than a Prezvaght builds in my mind, making my teeth chatter, but I don't argue with them. They're pointing something at us, which doesn't look exactly like a gun since it has eight fingers, but the way they're acting, we figure it must be dangerous. We walk forward in the direction they indicate.

We've been kept in a kind of fog so far, unable to see around us, but with their decision to take us the Craniums, whoever they are, the fog dissipates, and we can see the nature of the area where we've landed. It isn't inviting. For one thing, there's no Earth-like similarity to the ground cover.

What we can see looks like sand that sparkles with an ugly orangish hue, not at all like our tan and beige beaches. Or maybe it's more salmon-colored, rubbed with bits of redwood bark. Whichever, it undulates in a manner like calm ocean water, swaying and gurgling as if it is semi-live.

I raise my gaze to scan further. To say the far-off mountains and the closer sand dunes at a distance from us are hideous is an understatement. They are the nightmarish projections of a mentally insane artist.

The Prezvaght steer us toward what I guess is a vehicle, although it has legs and something that looks an awful lot like mandibles. In fact, the thing resembles an enormous hairless spider. Yet, when the men point their eight-fingered guns at us, Kaipor and I look at each other and, without a word, step up into its cavernous parts.

The two police/guard/soldier Prezvaght follow, then close the door. Almost immediately, the thing lights up inside, begins to vibrate, a bit like one of our walking escalators, and lifts up. The side where the Prezvaght sit has a window. I stare out through it and see the ginger-orange dunes rushing by.

"You will sit back," the more yellow of the Prezvaghts orders in an angry voice. I start to comply, but the other one argues with the first. For a moment, they speak together in Prezvaght. It surprises me that I can understand, but I don't ask Kaipor why. My mind is too numb from shock.

"The female carries a nurturing egg. Do not be rough with her," the splotchy green one says.

"But that is good. She will be juicier then,"

"She is Dirzaght, idiot. Have you lost your wits? They taste like grecik, and what is worse, make us ill if we attempt to digest them."

Mr. Yellow sighs. "But she looks human. She smells good, too."

"Ask the Craniums, then. Ask them if you may have the female for your taste buds. They will laugh in your face and then lock you up for your indiscretion. The Dirzaght have a treaty with us, remember?"

"What good is a treaty if they murder our species?" the yellow responds. "Besides, I prefer indigestion to unfulfilled revenge."

"What was the spy-operative to you? Why should you care if she is dead?"

During their argument, Kaipor is running his hand across my thigh. I stop his hand twice, but he continues. Then he leans over me. *Do not let on that you understand their language, my darling. Let that be our secret.*

I nod my head. We have not spoken out loud, but the green splotched Prezvaght somehow knows that we're communicating. "You over here," he demands, eyeing me. "Come." He pats the seat next to him.

I glance at Kaipor, asking him what I should do, but already, he's moved into protection mode.

"My *travmeb* cannot sit beside you. It is not allowed. Anyway, my proximity is necessary for the welfare of our baby. I'm sure you understand that."

It's obvious from the blank expression on the Prezvaght's face that he has no idea what Kaipor's talking about, but he nods his head and gives in to Kaipor's demand. Our ride continues without further words. Kaipor keeps his hand on my leg, making lazy circles. I don't understand the purpose, but for some reason, I lean back and relax.

Once more, the music, which has been playing on the edge of my notice, grows loud enough for us to hear more clearly. My head slowly lowers onto Kaipor's shoulder, and I drift off to sleep, still humming the wondrous melody.

When the spider contraption arrives at its stop, I wake up. Yawning, I start to stand, figuring that we'll be getting out, but that doesn't happen. Instead, another Prezvaght joins us. Then the spider lights up, lifts up, and scurries off. The extra Prezvaght sits beside the first two. He says nothing, just stares at us.

The music starts again, and I slide back against the seat, sleepily adjusting myself against Kaipor. I close my eyes. We stop a second time and again about an hour later. Each time, a Prezvaght joins us. The last two sit on the seat beside Kaipor.

It is warm inside the spider, and although the music is heavenly, the Prezvaghts, who always have a tendency to smell like sour cheese, grow rancid. The smell begins to nauseate me. I have not been ill for all the months of my pregnancy, but the rocky motion of the carriage and the odor of the alien bodies create an obstacle for diplomacy. I last as long as I can, and then I bolt up, saying, "Stop the coach. I have to get out."

"No, we can't allow that. What is the nature of your problem?" the green one demands.

"It's personal," I yell out, then I cover my mouth and fight against my urge to erupt. In a second, I continue. "If you don't let me out, I'm going to vomit all over you."

Perhaps the Prezvaght take a look at my face. Maybe it is the hand pressed over my mouth that convinces them, but for whatever reason, they stop the vehicle and open up the door. I pop out like a pebble from a slingshot. Then I crouch down in the orange soil, not a moment too soon for the upsurge that follows.

Kaipor is there, of course, beside me. He demands water, and they give it to him. Then he washes my face and hands and gives me some of the water to rinse out my mouth. Meanwhile, only the green-splotchy alien gets out of the coach. Holding a cloth over his mouth, he speaks with Kaipor for a moment. He comes closer to where I'm sitting, on top of a small boulder, breathing in and out with forced intensity.

"We must go on now," he tells me, wagging his many-fingered hand weapon.

I take one look at it and fling myself back to the ground. Eruption number two occurs.

After that, I have to pee, another time vexation for the eager-to-leave aliens. The yellowish Prezvaght climbs out of the vehicle to attempt to talk us back inside. He waves his weapon at Kaipor a bit, but my sweet *travmeb* shows Mr. Yellow the two places where I've been sick. The alien blues slightly and scurries back inside.

That's the last of the attempts to deal with a nauseated pregnant lady. No one else comes out to chat. Finally, Kaipor coaxes me back inside with the agreement that we trade places with the Prezvaghts, so I can sit beside the open window.

The spider lifts up, the music starts, and the Prezvaghts, all huddle together as if for warmth, pushing as far away from me as possible. Perhaps my clothes carry the remnants of my vomit.

It is late, pitch-dark, in fact when we arrive at our final destination. The group of buildings we have reached is very much like an old English castle except with ugly, salmon-colored rock walls dotted with vertically placed, short, pointy-looking spears that skirt its circular border.

Still in the spider-look-a-like vehicle, we pass through a portal. One would expect a draw bridge in front of a castle, but this has a long tunnel with windows in which we see guards stationed.

The thoroughfare we are traveling on appears to be the only path leading inward to the center of the fortifications. My eyes are riveted forward, wondering what our next sight will be, when I hear the bang of a gate banging shut behind us, a gate I never saw. Inside the tunnel we are passing through, lights flare on. I presume on automatic.

As we reach the end of the covered passage, a courtyard becomes visible. Weedy grasses cover the ground, but their presence brings no relief from the massive orangeness all around. A single stunted tree, with limbs distorted in an odd manner, grows in the middle. It wears no leaves, nor are there any on the ground. I wonder if it's dead.

Cylindrical turrets hold both guards and lighting, casting an aerie pallor over our path forward. Eyes glare down at us. Spears point outward in clawed hands.

Kaipor squeezes my hand. *It will be okay,* he tells me, but whether that mental whisper is reassurance for me or for himself, I do not know. I am certain that all his training for diplomacy has not included instruction on how to deal with being captured by the Prezvaght. I return his hand squeeze but say nothing.

The obscure light allows us to see adequately, but there is little to observe except the same sterile-looking barriers on all four sides. The orangish adobe-like walls appear to be seamless like poured concrete with the dye gone wrong.

I sigh heavily, wishing I were back at the Institute. My bed is calling to me. Fresh, clean sheets, warm blankets, a pillow to lay my head on, and, of course, Kaipor's arms around me. That would be so nice.

The music swells, changing its beat. Our path opens wider. The building we are aiming for appears close. With the shift in the music, the Prezvaght guards on the seat across from us straighten up and come alive, tugging and fixing their clothing. I glance at Kaipor, just about to tell him I have to go to the bathroom again when a trumpet blares out. I think we're being announced.

Then we stop. The spider lowers down, the lights and music go off, and the multi-fingered guns come back to point at us, indicating that we should get out.

Kaipor goes first and then helps me down, not that I need it, of course. I'm still spry and agile, even though my kidneys no longer allow long sits, and odd smells play havoc with my stomach. We're escorted inside through a series of tunnels wreathed by oval doorways. The Prezvaght guards surround us tightly, all smelling like the kind of French cheeses better left thoroughly wrapped in plastic. My nausea starts up again the moment we're enclosed in the stuffy building.

"Look, nothing personal," I tell Mr. Yellow, but if you don't find me a bathroom super-fast and give me some space, you're going to experience even more of what it's like to be pregnant. I'm about to erupt again."

You, my darling, are the sauciest wench I've ever known, laughs my travmeb. Very soon, you'll have the entire Prezvaght army trembling at your threats.

I don't know about that, but on the trip here, I apparently trained these ones well. The green-splotchy one steers me through a doorway and shuts me inside. The room is immense, much too big to be a bathroom, or so I think at first. But on exploration, I discover a Prezvaght using one of the toilets.

She is sitting down, her legs extended into the air. She doesn't react to the sight of me, doesn't even seem to notice my invasion. Obviously, she's intent on her own purpose for being there.

I walk on. There are no doors to provide anyone personal privacy, but I find a suitable seat with an opening in it and sample a Prezvaght toilet. I guess if you've used a toilet anywhere, they're more or less the same. I keep my feet off the leg rests and use this one in the standard human method. It works just fine. A splash of water on my face afterward relieves my nausea, at least without a horde of odorous guards surrounding me.

When I exit the room, no one is around. I walk up and down the hall, looking for them, but other than the blinking lights and the strange squiggly signs at the top of each wall, the place appears to be uninhabited.

"Come back here!" yells Mr. Yellow. He's alone except for his trusty finger gun. I ignore him and turn the next corner.

Bad idea. A whole squad of guards surround me, all of them with long poles that fall about me like I'm a beetle, finding myself in the middle of a game of Pick-Up-Sticks.

"She is my captive," the yellow bellows. The other five members of our group (including Kaipor) come running up. "Why did you not stay in the room you asked to visit?" Mr. Splotch demands.

"I used the facility. I didn't say I wanted to take up residency."

The platoon of pole carriers is still threatening us. Our group is standing them off. I fear that a battle is about to take place with Kaipor and me squished in the middle.

"What is this noise?" demands a great bellowing voice — think basset hound with an amplifier. When we turn to view him, we see that the roar is attached to a string bean of a giant Prezvaght, one who's leaning on a Prezvaght with no eyes.

"This is a personal matter that concerns the Council of Craniums," Mr. Splotch tells him, with a response that sounds slightly shaky from nervousness.

"I see," says the string bean. "Well, I am awake now. I shall call the others. This has caught my curiosity. I like this one's spirit. She is small but feisty and fertile. Good combinations for a noble female."

I guess the string bean is complimenting me, but I open my mouth to protest because I don't like the idea of being noble just because I'm fertile. That sounds sexist to me.

You will not argue with the Council of Craniums, my travmeb. Even you would not go that far, I hope, Kaipor says.

I have been dragged from my home, made to ride with over-ripe cheese, vomited everything I've eaten for the past two days, and been forced to share a bathroom with a Prezvaght. I am not in a good mood. I don't answer my *travmeb.*

We are led into a huge hall with masks hanging on every wall. Most of them look Halloweeny, but not in a fun way. String Bean motions us to sit. I glance around for a chair, a normal chair, but the only thing available are elephant feet with large, fluffy cushions. Kaipor and I sit.

Unfortunately, my stomach is complaining again. This time, I'm nauseated because my belly is empty. I sigh and look across at Kaipor, but he doesn't notice. He's watching the Craniums file in with the slow-measured footing of a group of brides walking down the church aisle.

A Prezvaght musician is accompanying the creatures' ponderous march, playing an enormous pipe-like stringed harp, which he not only blows into but uses his fingers to pull and push on a variety of strings and levers.

Really, I don't understand how such a primitive culture, one that craves meat enough to hop from planet to planet, devouring all the living creatures, can be cultured enough to make such beautiful music.

So you like our music but not our carnivorous ways? laughs String Bean, now sitting on an even larger chair than mine.

I would like you better if you would leave my world alone, I respond mentally, without diplomacy, perhaps, but with a great deal of honesty.

"Go closer," String Bean orders his chair.

As if it were alive, the elephant pedestal speeds its way toward me, scurrying rather like a spider vehicle on tentacle legs. Mine does the same, lurching like a drunken sailor.

We do leave your planet alone, String Bean responds, squiggling his eye sockets in a manner that I instinctively think is bafflement.

That takes me aback. I stare into his orange-circled eyes and attempt to understand why he would lie. Finally, I just blurt it out. *Don't bother making up idiotic stories. You killed my parents right in front of me and Danielle killed my friend just to be mean. Why bother to lie?*

String Bean studies me for a moment, tilting his head. Then he lets out a roar that reverberates across the room. Several respond in the same way. I don't understand the nature of their humor.

Meanwhile, Kaipor is tugging at his seat, trying to get it to move closer to mine. It won't lift up. It's as if it has been cemented to the floor.

"Please, order my *travmeb's* seat closer to me," I tell String Bean. "It refuses to cooperate with him."

The Prezvaght laughs and gives the command, and Kaipor, clinging to the sides of his chair to avoid falling off, gallops closer.

"Are you all right?" Kaipor asks the moment his chair settles down.

"Yes, but I'm really hungry. Now I'm getting sick because I have nothing in my stomach. It's an endless cycle."

Hungry? says String Bean. He claps his hands, orders food to be brought, then turns back to me. *Now, explain your last comment. I do not understand. We have never hunted on Dirzaght.*

Maybe that's true. I don't know, but I live on Earth. It was there you killed my parents and my friend.

Ah, our old breeding ground. Yes, we do have several lines there, which we keep for improving our farm-raised food sources. Those cattle were your friends? How is that possible?

The moment he calls them cattle, I burst up out of my chair. "How dare you say such a thing! You're nothing but murderers. What you do isn't legal, honorable, or even sane. Humans are people! They have the right to live without butchers from outer space descending on them. How can you be so cruel, so immoral, or so primitive?"

Kaipor moans loudly. String Bean almost falls off his chair, not from fear over my outburst but from laughter.

Meanwhile, Kaipor tries to calm me down, to get me to sit and let him handle it, but I'm so angry I'm fanning myself from the heat of my rage.

Are all Dirzaght women like this? String Bean asks my *travmeb*. *What a treasure! What a delight! No wonder you have chosen to breed her. If she breeds as true as . . .*

"Stop it! I am not a thing you can lift up and discuss," I yell, breaking away from Kaipor's hold.

With that, all the Craniums fall off their chairs and roll around the floor, clutching at their stomachs.

I'm about to throw something at them, at all of them, but then the food comes in. I grab at the nearest platter and stuff an unidentifiable biscuit into my mouth. It has the flavor of raw liver. Immediately, I spit it out into my hand. "Yuck! Don't you have anything that doesn't taste like meat?"

String Bean is just picking himself up off the floor. He stifles his laugh long enough to point to something that looks an awful lot like raw hamburger, and then he collapses once again, rolling around on the floor, clutching his stomach like he's been poisoned.

"That?" I gasp. "That isn't meat? What is it then?"

String Bean picks himself up, still holding onto his stomach, and attempts to give me an answer. "It's a local fruit," he finally tells me, repositioning himself on his chair, still bent over from belly laughing.

I pick up the odd-looking fruit thing and take a bite. Not bad. It tastes like an over-ripe pear, but at least it agrees with my stomach. I chew and swallow.

The Craniums adore you, my love, but that can change in an instant. Try not to anger them, my darling. Please.

Good advice, String Bean says. *Does she ever heed your guidance?*

"You can read Kaipor, too?" I ask after swallowing my second bite. "That's not nice, you know. What happened to your manners? Or don't you have any?"

Strata, that is enough. You will be silent now, Kaipor orders. I take another bite and think about it.

She does not talk like a Dirzaght. I sense that her heart is not there but with the Earthlings. What are these humans to her? Are they her pets? asks another of the Craniums, one sitting at the opposite side of the room.

"Don't be a fool! Humans aren't pets!" I protest.

Our women would make pets of all our prey if we allowed it, inserts another.

The children do, also. We must not forget the children, another adds.

"Humans are my friends!" I protest again.

Strata. Enough. You have made your point; now retreat, Kaipor warns again.

But our children grow out of it. Why has this one not done so? Is she very young still? asks the first one.

"You're not listening to me!" I shout at them.

I have warned you, my travmeb. *There will be no further warning,* Kaipor sends out so loudly that I turn and look at him.

His eyes are flaring. I open my mouth and shut it again. Then I sigh, watching him for a sign. Why has he ordered me to be silent? What have I said that has irritated him?

Yes, she is young, my travmeb says. *In Dirzaght, she will be considered a child-woman for a decade or more. One must constantly consider that she was raised by those you harvested. Since that time, she has floundered, unsure, and unled. Forgive her for her outbursts. I beg that you continue to see only her youthful zeal.*

String Bean issues a guttural hum, which makes it around the room. *Ah, we understand then. The youth are always impetuous. She is fortunate to have so tolerant a travmeb.*

I move my mouth and try to speak, but no sound follows. *Kaipor! This isn't fair. They want to hear from me!* I protest.

He reaches out and scoots me onto his lap. He wraps his arms around my body, then looks up at the Craniums. *I must take my travmeb back soon. What is it you want with us? We were not the ones who killed Danielle, the one masquerading as a human.*

Ah, you are right to return to the issue, String Bean nods approvingly. He reaches out for a biscuit like the one I sampled. His lips smack. His tongue licks. I gather he enjoys it.

We were so enchanted with your travmeb's audacity that we almost forgot the purpose of this meeting. Let the legal cross-examinations begin.

Splotched Green stands up and declares that he discovered me within six bismopos of the site of Danielle's death. Yellow verifies it.

Did she have a weapon in her hand? Was there evidence that she used one against our scout? String Bean asks.

Splotched Green looks over at me, then shakes his head. Yellow doesn't even glance my way. Instead, he says, *They are clever, these Dirzaght. They plead non-interference, but it is obvious that she was instrumental in the spy's death. She urged the human to shoot his antiquated weapon.*

What proof is there of this accusation? one of the Craniums in the back asks.

It is accumulative, my lord, says Splotched Green. *The human who fired had fallen to the ground, unable to bear the weight of his crime. It was obvious that this one . . .*

In what way was it obvious that the emotional one took part? Did you see her? Did you take note of the weapon exhaust on her hands? Did you see guilt in her eyes or hear words to that effect?

Splotched Green fades a bit at that rebuke. He glances over at me with the hint of a question in his eyes, although how I could tell that with his Prezvaght eyes circulating with orange and red highlights, I couldn't pinpoint.

No, my lord. I saw none of those things, but I believe that the Dirzaght are guilty. They were there. They must have taken part, he says in a voice deepened by shades of doubt.

I have finished my fruit and am looking for a second one. String Bean waves his hand, and another one glides over to my hand. I nod my thanks and bite in.

Meanwhile, Yellow is squirming like a toddler needing the toilet (or a pregnant woman?) *They are guilty!* he cries out, then checks with Splotched Green to see if Green has finished speaking. *This one,* he says, pointing to me, *is always in trouble. She is violent. I witnessed her throwing her food at another human, and I saw the male Dirzaght trip and kick a human.*

You waste our time. We do not care about their treatment of humans, a Cranium who has been silent until then says.

Yes, yes, so true, comes a chorus of Cranium voices.

This is all rubbish, anyway. The Dirzaght do not intercede, says the Cranium who mentioned pets.

The discussion's civility breaks down at that point. Green Bean has to call a Cranium *order in the court* to stop all the bickering.

This peek into the legal system on Prezvaght is all very interesting, but it is way past my bedtime. I cannot help letting out a huge yawn.

String Bean notices immediately. He studies me a moment, then calls for a halt in the proceedings.

The young mother is tired. We will adjourn tomorrow. Find a bedroom for the couple. We reconvene tomorrow at lunar four.

The next morning, there is more of the same. Yellow testifies, mostly what he has observed of unrelated events. Splotchy Green gives more of his pseudo evidence on the murder. The scene of the crime is discussed, and the Council of the Cranians talks on and on about justice and injustice and evidence and the lack of it.

Kaipor speaks often, but I'm not allowed. String Bean often reads into my mind, something I greatly dislike. He laughs when he does that and usually informs the others of my feelings, so I really don't understand the benefit of being speechless, but Kaipor says they are not the same thing at all. Kaipor tells me that thoughts cannot be used against me in the Prezvaght court but that spoken words can.

I suppose I should thank Kaipor for preventing me from speaking, but I cannot. I do not like the fact that he so often takes the upper hand in his dealings with me. The High Ones on Dirzaght would not approve either, I think. I shall ask them next time. Maybe.

In the end, the Prezvaght decide in my favor. Neither Kaipor nor I are blamed for the death of the agent. A celebratory drink is passed around to all involved at the conclusion of the trial. When it is my turn to take a sip, Kaipor starts to forbid me to drink, but String Bean says that I must. I take a small sip. When I have done so, String Bean toasts me, saying actually rather nice things about me.

Since the proceeding has gone so well, Kaipor returns my voice, and I am free to speak about my belief that it is wrong for Prezvaght to hunt humans. I tell the Prezvaght all the wondrous things I've learned about humans and about why humanity deserves to prosper. I rant on also about the things Danielle did to us and how she told me another would come in her place.

Is that true? one of the Prezvaght in the back row asks.

If it is, cancel it, says String Bean. *The agent, Danielle, has put this one through enough stress. We do not wish the baby to be born early. The Dirzaght would be furious with us if we caused that.*

"Please, you won't allow my friends to be hurt anymore, will you?" I plead. "I know you watch me. You've always done so. But why should my friends suffer just because of what I did?"

String Bean once again shows surprise at my words. His orange eyes stop their revolution, and he stares at me. Then he turns to check with the others. *Have we been monitoring this one? Has she fallen under our watch?*

Splotchy Green opens up a huge volume they say is called *Research* and finds my name listed there. I have an orange marker for my role in intervening in the attack on my parents. Yellow argues that it's well deserved and that the Prezvaght must continue to revenge their honor on me.

"You were cowards to attack my parents. They were defenseless," I cry out in justification.

Stars! Don't you have one iota of common sense, Strata? Kaipor demands as he claps two fingers together. *No more talking, my darling. I can't allow you to speak your way into some horrid Prezvaght punishment.*

Forgive her. She is as emotional as all young and, even worse, has learned no skills of diplomacy, Kaipor then tells the appalled Council of Cranians.

She amuses us, it is true, but her behavior is not Dirzaght, String Bean scolds Kaipor sharply. *Have you not yet commenced her instruction?*

Kaipor sighs heavily. His arm has already corralled me, but he pulls me closer and gives me a hug and a kiss on my forehead. *I have not been able to. As I told you, my travmeb is still just a child. You took away her parents. She had no one to teach her. She has not fully recuperated from that. Would you punish a child for lacking the proper knowledge?*

You see, until recently, my travmeb had no memories of Dirzaght. She was intended to be our test case, our collector. We gave her a blank slate to provide us with unbiased accounts. But then your hunting party emotionally injured her, and our plans for her were necessarily altered.

String Bean nods. *I see,* he says, staring at me again, his pupils once more rotating, but slower and with the beat of his thoughts.

You admired her courage the day before, Kaipor continues. *When you took her parents, was she not as bold then? Look up her valor on that day. You will find it equally admirable as her bravery yesterday. She was only a small tot, standing up to a troop of Prezvaght warriors, fighting a lost cause. Everyone knows that the Prezvaght value courage. Do you not honor it and reward its virtue?*

Five chairs scurry down from their high positions. Their riders search my face at a proximity that makes me want to scream.

He took away her voice when she did not listen. He is obviously training her, the first one says, his chair taking him the closest. *Yet he cannot take away her light. Her eyes resist. She has Prezvaght eyes. See them?*

Her thoughts, too. And she is not as ugly now as when she first arrived. Actually, she shows promise. She will bear him a fine son.

I'm about to pop off for that remark when I remember I have no voice. I sigh and glower at Kaipor, thoroughly dismayed that I'm still mute and must endure such insults.

String Bean laughs. *Mother-child, your travmeb is wise. He protects you. Your thoughts are scorching. They would lead you down a dark lane into a quagmire of trouble.*

The others nod and laugh among themselves. My face grows hotter.

Then what do we do? asks another. *Do we bar ourselves from Terra? Do we exclude a perfectly delicious species of flesh from our table?*

I jump up to make some angry gestures about his question, but Kaipor is ready for my response. His arms pull me back down into his lap. I can only glare my thoughts, then.

Her skin and her feelings are both soft, Kaipor explains. *You would find that distasteful in your women, but for us it is a quality much admired. I ask that you not injure her more with your words. Leave her the planet that fills her heart. You have many. Let her be unobserved, remembering that she was and is still only a child. Reward her bravery.*

Well spoken, Dackor of the Dirzaght Peacekeepers. We will discuss this among ourselves. Leave us now.

When Kaipor and I exit the room, my voice comes back. "Why did you do that? I only spoke the truth. It wasn't fair . . ."

I protect you always, Strata. You know that. You have no training yet. You say whatever comes into your mind. That is not wise.

I have decided that when we return, I shall begin your instruction in the ways of the Dirzaght. You will learn to self-monitor by applying the rules. Together, we shall work on tongue self-adjustment. Then when you are able to guide yourself with this problem, I shall no longer need to take away your voice. Do you understand?

"When I do it your way, then you will allow me to speak?"

He laughs. *You will not bait me, my dear. If that is the way you see it, then I will accept your version. But my description, I would think, would be easier for you to stomach. You are to teach yourself to moderate. That is all. Self-help, my darling. It is for your benefit and to keep you from being thrown into alien dungeons.*

Due to Kaipor's diplomacy (and possibly my bold speeches,) the Prezvaght cancel their private war with me and vow to leave Earth alone.

Even though I can't change their cultural position about murdering innocents, at least I'm more or less over my own personal horror of them. I still consider them the gangsters of the universe and believe that killing for food is a crime, but having observed the Prezvaght's legal system and listened to their music, I know I'll never think of them in the same way.

I guess it's true that one's opinion can radically change upon meeting and getting to know the enemy.

String Bean sends Kaipor and me off the following day with a military salute and a shared drink in tribute. He laughs and gives us a comedy act about his career, which is more satire than hilarious. We find that he's not really an evil sort.

The blind man he leans on even winks at us. String Bean admits that my visit has been an educational experience for the Council of Craniums. Then he starts laughing again, sliding down onto the floor.

When he gets up, we thank him and climb into the same or similar spider conveyance that we used to travel to the Palace.

On the way to the launch site, Splotched Green and Yellow, who are once again accompanying us, discuss their family and their children's game playing. I wonder about what Prezvaght kids look like. I've never seen any young ones.

My thoughts are picked up by Splotchy. He digs out a couple of the latest Prezvaght technology marvels — holographic videos — and displays his teen son and two adult daughters.

Mr. Yellow has nothing comparable. Both his computers have been down for weeks, he tells us. But he explains that his four children are all adults who have not yet presented him with grandchildren, something he appears to be deeply dissatisfied with.

Then, he proceeds to describe the strange animal that his wife has adopted. She has even started taking the *fopret* to pet shows, and the animal's grooming and training have become her newest hobby. She is so enthused with the pet, Mr. Yellow says, that she has begun to craft a miniature bonsai in the shape of her *fopret*.

As Yellow tells us this, his eyes flash with strange lights, and his pupils streak rapidly up and down in diagonal lines. I have learned that such is an indicator of deep passion and love. Two weeks ago, I would not have believed a Prezvaght could ever experience love. I glance at Kaipor, and he squeezes my hand.

As coincidental as life often is, Splotchy latches onto the conversation and begins to give us How-to Advice. It seems that he has studied the genealogy of his own pet *fopret* and is writing a biographical novel with the *fopret* as the main character.

He gives us a brief history so we'll understand the storyline, but I'm afraid that neither Kaipor nor I am paying much attention until he reaches the part where he relates his discovery that all *foprets* are homosexuals.

How do they reproduce, then? I ask. *Isn't that rather a biological impossibility?*

Nature is full of mystery, Yellow responds. *When the health of the* fopret *is good and the time for parenting arrives, it forms a short-termed relationship — no romance or love, you understand — but the relationship does the job. Then, the fopret returns to its preferential state and continues its emotional attachment to the originally chosen mate.*

Yellow begins to tell us about the mating dance, but I become uncomfortable with the conversation. *Could we talk about something else?* I ask timidly.

The Prezvaghts laugh, but they oblige me. One of them, I think it is Yellow (My face is hot, and I'm too embarrassed to look up to see,) asks us a joke. Why did the flea flee?

Neither Kaipor nor I know the answer. We shrug and watch Splotchy slide off the seat because he's laughing so hard. I figure it must be a really good joke, but when Yellow gives us the answer: The flea flew fleetingly by flicking his flimsy flippers after filching the flirtatious, fletching, and feisty Mrs. Fly.

Kaipor and I just look at each other and then politely laugh. So much for Prezvaght humor.

We stop several times on the way to the Vortex Port to allow me to water the salmon-colored sand, but otherwise, our method of transportation is fleet and direct as an arrow. We nibble on the food we've brought along in a picnic basket and hear more of the Prezvaght "jokes."

Then the Prezvaghts tell us about an environmental problem they've been having in the area we're passing through, which floods constantly. We're discussing that while munching cookies (which are especially sublime). The subject leads Mr. Yellow to admit that he read a story of mine about ecology that I posted online in my writing portfolio.

I'm surprised that he's even heard of the site, and I question him about it. Splotchy looks embarrassed, but he finally admits that they perused the Internet, making the Web a part of their daily reports about me.

"So you read my stories?" I ask.

"Oh, absolutely. My favorite one was the one about the ghost and using the Ouija board to solve the case. Nice touch," Splotchy tells me.

Kaipor smiles, as pleased as I am. Then he says, *When Strata returns to Dirzaght, I am hoping she will be interested in writing more stories about Earth. Such tales would fascinate our world.*

That's an idea I've never considered. I could be a writer on Dirzaght. Maybe I could tell the Dirzaght about the Prezvaght and our trip to the Cranium court, about the Leoreons, and of course, as Kaipor has said, about Earth.

The thought of doing that makes my approaching move to Dirzaght a lot less objectionable. I give Kaipor a smile and a quick kiss. I would very much like to be a foreign journalist/story teller.

As we continue chatting on our travel in the spider coach, I learn that Splotchy and Yellow have been with me throughout my entire stay at the Institute. They rode the bodies of the various humans around me. No wonder I saw Prezvaght everywhere I looked. That was the main reason I thought I was crazy.

I wasn't. That knowledge brightens everything.

When we reach the vortex, we part. I realize that my fear of the Prezvaght has completely disappeared. Kaipor and I climb into the vortex and wave goodbye.

Lift-off is immediate. It speeds Kaipor and me directly into the sky. This time, we have a moment to talk.

So many things have changed, I tell my travmeb.

Kaipor's arms tighten around me. *Yes, too many,"* he says. *We will go back to the Institute now so that you can say goodbye to your friends, my darling, but I'm pulling you from your position there. The Prezvaght kidnapped you. I now have just cause to present to the Council.*

But I'm not ready to go, I argue.

You will never be ready, Strata. You are Dirzaght, but when questioned by the Prezvaght, you were confused by your true identity. You must learn to know who you are now, my darling. You must learn your true heritage so we can teach it to our son.

The vortex sets us down then, not in the dining room, which is where we'd left from, but in my bedroom. I'm glad of that. I shower, dress, and comb my hair.

"How much time has elapsed?" I ask.

We have gone back in time again, my dear. Melanie still lives. She and the others are waiting for you downstairs. Let this be brief, darling. You may say goodbye to your friends, but it would be pointless to tell your doctors. They would not understand or believe your words.

I nod. As we walk down the stairs, I know I'll never come back, not to the Institute, anyway, because I no longer need it.

Chapter Fifteen

I look into our den room. Zoey is sitting on the couch. Chris is with her. They look happy. I run to her and kiss her cheek. "I'm leaving with Kaipor," I say. "I'm going home, and I won't be back. I just wanted to tell you goodbye. I'll miss you."

Chris starts to get up. He doesn't accept my words and wants to call a doctor, but Zoey calms him down. "It's for the best," she tells Chris. "Don't you see? It's where Clea has always belonged."

Melanie is lucid that day. She rises and walks toward me. "You are choosing a fresh start," she says. "I wish I could do that." She had been sitting on the old brown couch. It was often her favorite place, shaggy and depressing as it was. It was where she spent so much of her gone time, where she slipped into the void of nothingness.

I turn to look at Kaipor, but he shakes his head. He knows what I'm thinking about giving her that fresh start.

Kaipor unblurs himself so that all three of them can see him fully. Chris is stunned and silent. His eyes suddenly look like Melanie's when she zombies out. Zoey will help him. She'll allow him to fold back into disbelief, to ignore what he is seeing now. She'll be his anchor of reality. We all need one of those. Without one, we end up here in the Institute, unstrapped and wild with our visions. Swaying like seaweed as the assaults of pain crush us.

Melanie is attempting to anchor to me, like she had with Danielle. Her fingers affix themselves to me, clinging tightly. She has no one else to hold onto. She doesn't spend enough time in reality to dig her feet into solidity. I cannot brush her away. Her need is too great.

"I am destined for death here," Melanie breathily cries out, "Take me with you, please." Her eyes plead with Kaipor. She knows that I have already given in to her plea that I am willing to be her support.

Yes, I agree. We can buoy each other in this new world we're going to. I have Kaipor. He can be my foundation, my roots, but having a friend would make everything so much easier for Melanie and for me.

"You won't die now," Kaipor says. "You can live without fear. Clea has removed your danger."

Melanie sees that Kaipor is still trying to refuse her. She shakes her head, then turns her wrist, and we see the lines. She has tried to cut herself many times in seeking death. She will soon find it on her own unless she has another escape. She is alive only because she has not yet found an instrument sharp enough to end her days.

The sight horrifies me. My heart breaks. I look into her eyes and see an ocean of overwhelming sadness. I know then that I cannot leave her behind. Someone must help her to sanity. The psychiatrists and all the drugs in the world cannot fix her. Rape has destroyed her. It has stolen her life.

Perhaps Kaipor reads my thoughts, my unwillingness to leave Melanie behind.

"She is Terran, my love. It would be too hard for her to adapt," Kaipor tells me gently, but Melanie throws her arms around me. Her tears sting my face.

"I will succeed at death if you are not here," she tells me.

I straighten my shoulders. "Kaipor, we have to take her with us. I demand it from the Council for services rendered."

My *travmeb* sighs. He is still shaking his head again, but his refusals are less. He is bending to me, accepting that he must.

"Are you positive, my darling one? You will soon have our son. He will take your time. As will the books you wish to write."

Melanie and I have entwined our hands. Both of us nod our heads. She looks buoyant, her eyes, for once, clear and filled with hope. I could never turn away from her now.

Kaipor merely stands a moment more, shaking his head, perhaps pondering this new difficulty that I wish to saddle him with. Then he emits a heavy sigh, squeezes my shoulder, and says, *Life will never be boring with you, my travmeb. We will take her with us. The Council will yell. The High Ones will lecture, but it seems our fate is to be in trouble with the ruling groups. So be it.*

Carmen put down her book to join us. Although she'd been in the other room, content as always, she'd heard our conversation. "This is good. I knew you didn't belong here, Clea, but it was fun while it lasted. We will miss you," she says, turning so she includes both Melanie and me. She hugs us and wipes a tear.

The Institute's men have dribbled in, their eyes fixated on Kaipor. I fear that his silver face might upset their equilibrium, but they don't react like sane people. They merely accept that reality buckles and churns. They nod to him and circle us, friendly as tail wagging puppies.

Joe, who is puzzlingly not in prison, but is back amidst us, comes closer. "So, your alien is real after all."

I nod. "And we're leaving now, going home to Dirzaght."

My words please Kaipor. He smiles and kisses my cheek. His arm around my shoulder tightens as if making a declaration to Joe once and for all.

"It is time to go," Kaipor states firmly.

Melanie inches closer, bonding herself to me so that Kaipor's arms can circle both of us. The vortex drops down, neutralizes our body shape, then lifts us. As we rise into space, Kaipor's dream horse gallops toward us.

My *travmeb,* floating in the air as if doing so is a normal thing to do, lifts Melanie onto the horse's long, wide back. He places me at the front and then boosts himself up to squeeze in between us. At his request, Melanie wraps her arms around his waist, and I contentedly lean back into my *travmeb's* strong, secure arms.

We are ready then. The sky horse charges forward and leaps upward into the stars, carrying us, at long last and forever, to our new home on Dirzaght. My dreams of college fade into the past. My many sessions of psychiatry slip into the mists of memory. Goodbye computer, my niche of a room, and the Institute where I was enclosed so long in my pseudo haven of self-doubt.

But none of that matters any longer. My beloved *travmeb* will be at my side, no longer hidden, no longer a secret. Melanie and I will get our reward for the horrors we've both experienced. We'll see a world with oddities, adventures, and the kind of peace unobtainable on Earth. I will meet my son, Threll, soon, and finally, I'll understand all the mysteries of Dirzaght.

This time, as I fly home, no fear stabs my heart. I smile in anticipation, finally eager for the bright, clean beginning that awaits not just me but Melanie, Kaipor, and our son.

As the horse carries us across the stars, I recall Carthian's words. I had rejected them sharply, hurt that he had made it all seem like an eraser could rub out hardship and grief. I'd refused his advice then. But now I saw that he was right. Time did soften some of the BAD, enough that we could climb out of the abyss and press forward.

I no longer cared about revenging my uncle, what happened to Tom, the mistakes I'd made, or my lost years of childhood. There is recovery after the BAD.

"You must just pull yourself out. It's that's simple," Carthian had told me that day, and I'd felt a moment of hate for such simplicity. But there was also a choice. I could continue feeling sorry for myself, for all the evil in my life. I could even be like Melanie, seeking Death as my answer. Or, I could look to the future and make it *my* choice to find happiness.

I would help Melanie to see that choice, too. We could support each other in our new lives, climbing our way into the sunlight.

Perhaps simple wasn't what Carthian should have said. Dealing with tragedy was never simple. Maybe what he should have said is that we have a choice.

Threll began kicking. Was he celebrating his homecoming? Did he know that everything was about to open into a new vista?

As the horse landed and we stepped into the loving embrace of the Dirzaghts, who were finally welcoming us home permanently, I smiled. No one seemed disgusted by the sight of Melanie. They enveloped her in a series of loving embraces, sheltering her and bolstering her as if they had known her always.

The women surrounded Kaipor, as well, soothing his angst. My poor *travmeb* must have been fearful of what the Elders would do to him. I realized that I had given him an extra burden by insisting that my friend come with us. Just like in the past, I had hampered his diplomacy and forced him into making apologies for my combative verbal outpourings.

I would accept his training and let his teachings modify my impulses. At least, I would try. Like the academics I had been stuffing into my brain, I realized that there were many modalities for learning.

So, it was a new world, one that still felt alien to me, as it would for a while, but it was a good reality, and my choices had been made.

The women were guiding us to the baths. I recognized the direction. I wasn't opposed to feeling the warm waters with their scents of comfort, but for the moment, I stopped and turned. A face I recognized had halted my progress.

It was Carthian, the Dirzaght who had helped me before. When he saw my gaze, he bowed his head. Then he smiled.

"It is as simple as that," I heard him say, although he was a good distance away. I returned his gesture, but when I looked up, he was gone.

Kaipor took my hand and gently tugged me forward. Melanie, on the other side of me, giggled. I had never heard her laugh before.

A new beginning. A good beginning. It was as simple as that.